Of **KINGS** *and* **Fools**

Of Kings and Fools

Stories of the French Tradition in North America

Collected, translated, and retold by

Michael Parent
and Julien Olivier

August House Publishers, Inc.
LITTLE ROCK

14851792

Published by August House, Inc.,
P.O. Box 3223, Little Rock, Arkansas, 72203,
501-372-5450.

Note to Storytellers: We'd be delighted if you told the folktales in this collection. We'd also appreciate it if you sent your listeners to this book. However, please let us tell the personal and family stories and remember that the authors' and publisher's permissions are required for the reprinting or recording of any of these stories.

Printed in the United States of America

10 9 8 7 6 5 4 3 2 1 PB

LIBRARY OF CONGRESS CATALOGING-IN-PUBLICATION
Parent, Michael.
Of kings and fools : stories of the French tradition in North America / collected,
translated, and retold by Michael Parent and Julien Olivier.
p . cm.
Includes bibliographic references.
ISBN 0-87483-481-3 (pbk. : alk. paper)
1. French-Americans—Folklore. 2. French-Canadians—Folklore.
3. Tales—Northeastern States. I. Olivier, Julien. II. Title.
GR111.F7 1996   1996
398.2'089114074—dc20   96-24379

President and publisher: Ted Parkhurst
Executive editor: Liz Parkhurst
Project editor: Suzi Parker
Cover design: Harvill Ross Studios Ltd.
Production assistant: Ira L. Hocut
Assistant editor: Sarah Scott

This book is printed on archival-quality paper which meets the guidelines for performance and durability of the Committee on Production Guidelines for Book Longevity of the Council on Library Resources.

AUGUST HOUSE, INC.   PUBLISHERS   LITTLE ROCK

To Alice, Gerard, and Norman Parent. (M.P.)

To Jane and Jennifer, Nicole, Danielle, and Anique,
our four daughters who inherit
and pass on our traditions. (J.O.)

Acknowledgments

✚✚✚✚✚✚✚✚✚✚✚✚✚✚✚✚

To my papa, Gérard Parent (1912-83), and my mama, Alice Fournier Parent (1918-95), who talked, sang, and gave me stories in French. To my brother, Norman, a good papa who always reads bedtime stories to Mikie and Stephanie.

To my grandparents, Ferdinand and Adeline Parent, and Honoré Fournier, who spoke to me in French and thus gave me a fine reason to keep speaking it. To my grand-mother, Stephanie Fournier, who, though she died before I was born, I was able to know through many stories told about her.

To Imelda and Joe, Antoinette and Ray, Lucille and Phil, Beatrice and Joe, and to the many other aunts, uncles, and cousins who've given me the feeling I'm part of a large, story-filled tribe.

To my buddies: Blumos and many others.

To Heather Forest for the idea of doing this book.

—Michael Parent

To Alice, Marcel, Noël, and all who told me some of the happier family stories.

To Anna, Jim, Omer, Émile, and countless others who made the oral tradition come alive in our interviews.

—Julien Olivier

To Franco-Americans, the Northeast's "Quiet Presence" as one author calls them. They have lived their culture for four centuries.

To reseachers, publishers, lovers of oral traditions, and publishing houses who helped us: Sandy Ives of the

Archives of Oral History and Folklore of the University of Maine; Jean-Claude Dupont of the Département d'histoire, Université Laval; and Les Éditions Beauchemin of Montréal.

And to those now deceased grand-daddies of the oral tradition in Québec and among Franco-Americans of New England: Luc Lacourcière, Adelard Lambert, and Marius Barbeau. Merci.

To Suzi Parker, our editor, for acting as a clear-sighted "third eye."

Finally, to Liz and Ted Parkhurst and the people of August House, who've made the business of publishing books a warm art. *(M.P. and J.O.)*

Contents

Regarding Dialect and the Glossary

✦✦✦✦✦✦✦✦✦✦✦✦✦✦✦✦✦

To readers who are fluent in or familiar with French, please note that we're working with a regional dialect that is spoken in parts of Québec and the northeastern United States. This dialect or flavor of French is as different from "standard French" as American English is from that spoken in London. This flavor of French is the one we grew up hearing and speaking. It contains the kinds of quirks and eccentricities that make languages as well as the people who speak them so endlessly unique and fascinating.

To give readers some help in following our dialect and language, we have included a glossary of terms both standard and dialectic. The words in italics can be found in the back of the book beginning on page 189. Where confusion could occur or long passages are in French, we have placed the English translation in parenthesis beside the French.

Introduction

History says ...
Franco-Americans of today descended from hardy explorers who plied the seas between Brittany or Normandy and "New France" (Canada) in the sixteenth and seventeenth centuries. They are the off-spring of those who risked all, sailing across the Atlantic Ocean and trying their luck in a new and often brutal land. Once established in Canada, some of these early settlers continued traveling as explorers and trappers—they became *voyageurs* and *coureurs de bois*. These adventurers trekked the vast continent across the Great Lakes and the towering mountains to the far West, down the rivers and through the huge territory named *Louisiane* in honor of King Louis XIV.

Their progeny are the people who, in the late nineteenth century, when economic conditions made life intolerable on the farm, headed south to build new homes and new lives *aux États*, where the textile mills, powered by the mighty rivers of New England, were running full force. Half of Québec was displaced in the process.

Very few Americans are aware of this history. Yet, according to the 1990 census, the northeastern United States is home to more than three million people of French heritage.

Michael says ...
My mother's family, the Fourniers, journeyed from Québec to Suncook, New Hampshire, and finally to Lewiston, Maine. My grandfather, Honoré Fournier, eventually became an overseer in the rayon weaving room at the

Bates Manufacturing Co. textile mills. My father's family followed a similar route, leaving Québec for Salmon Falls, New Hampshire, and then traveled to Lewiston, where my paternal grandfather, Ferdinand Parent, worked as a tailor.

My early childhood revolved around two things: the tailor shop that my *pepère* and papa operated in downtown Lewiston and visits to Memère and Pepère Parent's house "out in the country" on Bailey Avenue. About three miles from the center of town, it was the family gathering place on Sundays and special occasions where the latest news, jokes, and stories were told—mostly in French.

The tailor shop occupied the front room of our first-floor apartment on Middle Street, aptly named since we were within shouting distance of the most important places in town. The Bates Street playground was a half-block away. So was the Central Fire Station where my friends and I watched the fire trucks scream out to fires and were lucky enough to be their official "backer-uppers" when they returned. As long as we stood in our designated safe spots, the firemen let us wave the drivers back into the huge garage. We added vocal authority to our expert "backer-upping" by repeating "Back up, Dixie Cup!" until we had guided those sparkling behemoths into their appointed places.

The cathedral-like Saints Peter and Paul's Church stood a block and a half up Ash Street from the firehouse and could be seen for miles around. Saints Peter and Paul's School, imposing but not as majestic as the church, sat three blocks up Bates Street.

Most of the inhabitants of this little world spoke French, but I don't remember giving that much thought as a child. Through the years, in my travels as a performer, I've met countless people who know of my French-Canadian heritage. But unless I tell them otherwise, they often assume that since I've spoken French since childhood and because I continue to do so, I must have grown up in Québec and later moved to the United States.

In fact, my grandparents, like the grandparents of many people of French heritage in New England, came to the United States by way of French Canada. Their ancestors had settled in the area known as Acadia (today's Maritime Provinces) and in Québec. In migrating South, our grandparents' generation intended to come to the States only briefly, make some money, stay out of trouble, and move back home. They did not make a lot of noise—in public anyway. They banded together in their neighborhoods, spoke French, occasionally kicked up quite a ruckus singing and dancing, and otherwise mostly stayed to themselves.

So it is not surprising that even today few Americans know of the Franco-Americans and their culture. Like cautious visitors unwilling to offend a powerful host, these immigrants were reluctant to be the center of attention in a stranger's house. Their songs and stories were sung and told around their own fires but not when strangers or "the boss" were around.

Why, I asked myself as a younger man, didn't my grandparents' and parents' generations manage to preserve their native French-speaking culture and at the same time assimilate into the larger English-speaking culture?

Why, specifically, were they not able to mix with the strangers or shed their *Canuck* accents *and* speak French and English equally well?

The answer came to me gradually and only many years later. They did not because they could not. They had another, more fundamental job to do, one that consumed most of their energies. That job was survival. I realized that I was the one who should be doing the very thing I wanted them to do—telling stories. I should because I could, and

I can precisely because they did their job. My grandparents and parents made this journey and built a new life—and also managed to preserve their heritage—in a strange place. Now I have the opportunity to tell the stories they couldn't tell and sing the songs they couldn't sing—in both French and English. I can also choose to sing them and tell them around any fire.

This book is an attempt to thank those hardy, loving people for doing their "job." And also to celebrate them not only for surviving but for telling me the stories and singing me the songs—and thus clearing the path for me to make the journey to my own "job."

Julien says ...

The priest towered over his audience. His voice and physical stature were riveting and magnetic. From one story to the next, he wove an evening filled with heroes, mythical beings, and talking animals. I sat at his feet enthralled with the sound of his voice. A powerful preacher, Alphonse Breault—priest, missionary, and healer—would exercise outside the pulpit this second vocation of *raconteur*. I think many of the thousands who attended his mission retreats in New England's Franco-American churches did so to be allowed into the soirées de rire, or evenings of laughter, that followed Breault's sometimes hell-and-brimstone deliveries in the pulpit.

This storyteller-preacher, known as *le bon* Pére Breault, the good Father Breault, followed a long succession of French-Canadian and Franco-American *raconteurs*, men and women who kept alive not only the stories but the dreams and aspirations, the fears and taboos, the joys and the awe of a people. *Raconteurs* were not only the bearers of tradition, they were the entertainment of their day. I also have the impression that *raconteurs* were not self-taught but were born into the tradition.

It is getting more and more difficult to find people like Père Breault and Émile Lévesque of Augusta, Maine, another storyteller of the old tradition. At the age of ninety-one, Émile is a direct link to the past: his father, generations of storytellers, the Québec town of Trois-Pistoles, and, lastly, France. Even today, his family still gathers around the elderly man to hear stories.

I grew up in an atmosphere of oral tradition. French songs (the *voyageurs* tunes, first sung here by men who navigated the great rivers of the United States), recipes (some used daily, others for holidays), folk wisdom (*Le trois fait le mois*/The third day sets the weather pattern for the whole month) ... this still was the essence of everyday life in the 1940s and 1950s—all passed on by word-of-mouth. The ancient tales appeared to be fading even then, and few and far between were families like the Breaults and the Lévesques.

So it was at home that I heard over and over again how Pepère Alexis Lacasse, my mother's father, had been the last of fifteen children, born to parents already in their fifties, orphaned as a child, with no where to go but to "the States." I learned how Maria, his once young and beautiful bride, had come from Trois-Rivières with her sister Anna to work in the mills of Manchester, New Hampshire. I knew that no matter how hard life was in the mills, back on the farm in Canada life was worse. There was the cousin whose mother had died and whose father spent the entire winter in a far-away logging camp. Chopping a hole in the ice, this eldest son saw to the sanitary needs of his siblings by washing them in the frigid Canadian waters.

I also relived vicariously the tragedy of my grandfather Alexis's death at age forty-four, leaving a widow and twelve children. The year was 1935, the height of the depression, and the very same year the Amoskeag mills closed their doors. But I also knew that Pepère Olivier, having been born in the United States, had succeeded in purchasing a home and owning his own business, The Olivier 5-Cent Cigar. Family stories were at the heart of everyday life. They belonged to no one and to everyone. Undoubtedly, a lesson could be learned from these stories.

I have often been disappointed that Franco-American folklore does not include great myths of creation, or of good and evil. I confess a certain envy for native peoples whose stories I love. These tales seek to explain the deeper truths of existence. We Franco-Americans share in the Judeo-Christian story-heritage common to many, and—whether we consider ourselves religious or not—our perceptions of reality are influenced by biblical world views.

Despite this mythical deficiency, our stories—the tales, legends, and family histories—still do offer insight into our selves and psyches. Most often our stories turn to laughter. Perhaps, that cheapest of medicines was our ancestors' way of healing the soul if not the body. Perhaps Père Breault healed as much in his *soirées de rire* as when he administered a relic and prayed over the sick. Perhaps, in an age of dwindling medical coverage, we ourselves need to rediscover the healing power of storytelling.

We say ...

Some of these stories are personal. We've cooked them up based on family experiences or recounted them as we heard them. Others, we have translated. But in all cases, we assume the responsibility of their retelling.

We are indebted to many people—some because they were caretakers and bearers of the tradition through the centuries; others, for having been collectors of stories; finally to all who actually passed them on to us. Many of these stories might well have been lost years ago if not for the painstaking, lifelong efforts of folklorists like Lambert, Barbeau, and Lacourcière.

Pick Up and Go— to a Place We Can Call Chez-Nous

⚜⚜*⚜*⚜*⚜*⚜*⚜*⚜*⚜*⚜*⚜*⚜*

The usual immigrant experience, which involved being forced or compelled to leave the homeland because of religion, politics, famine, or economic opportunity, often meant that those who made the voyage most likely would not return to their birthplace. European immigrants usually crossed the Atlantic Ocean only once. French-Canadians, however, could leave their homeland, cross the border into the United States, and quite easily return to Québec or to Acadia, today known as the Maritime Provinces of Canada. And that was often their intention. Many families crossed the border with hopes that their strong work ethic and many work-eligible children would help them to make enough money to revive sagging farms. Whether they eventually went back or not, that lingering possibility molded their behavior. It slowed their assimilation into the "new culture" and moved them to replicate their "old life"—as nearly as they could—by banding together in French-speaking neighborhoods called Petits-Canadas.

Chez nous *refers not only to a person's own house and home, but to that place where he or she feels most like they "belong," where they are surrounded by people whose love, understanding, and acceptance are unconditional. Some French-Canadians (among the nearly 1.5 million who made the trek south) left in an attempt to salvage their "old" lives, to work hard so that they could return* chez nous *as soon as possible; others left looking for "new" lives, to find better homes, and build new* chez nous. *Very few left because they yearned to wander as nomads. Most were simply searching for a treasured* chez nous.

Even after they settled into their jobs as mill-hands and appeared very sedentary, these descendants of the voyageurs still brimmed with the old traveling spirit. The invention of the automobile and the passage of legislation that provided workers with more leisure time also encouraged that same pick-up-and-go spirit.

Ready to Go—
Even in Your Sleep
Toujours prêts à partir

"Know thyself."
"How shall I?"
"Listen to the stories of those who love you." (M.P)

I'd never seen an actual king. Lewiston, Maine, wasn't likely to be on a king's itinerary. But when my *pépere*, Honoré Fournier, showed up for a visit with only a pocket watch and chain as adornment, it always felt to me like a king had indeed arrived.

After he retired from the textile mills, he spent much of his time "visiting." He had started out in the mills sweeping floors and worked his way up to the important position of overseer. So Pepère retired with a good pension. And since his wife, Stephanie, my grandmother, had died, he was on his own and pretty much did as he wanted. What pleased him most was traveling all over New England, visiting his family, spending his money on "havin' a damn good time," or giving "pay me back when you can" loans to a family member who'd lost a job or who'd found a house but not the down payment. If anyone objected to his generous, kingly ways, he'd say, "Let's spend the money now, have some fun, and you won't have to fight over it when I kick the bucket!"

He also liked to spoil his grandchildren and felt it was part of his job description as a *pepère*. He enjoyed sending his grandchildren out for ice cream with more than enough money and telling them, when they returned with what they thought was a king's ransom, to keep the change. This, of course, led to some disagreements between "the king" and his daughter and son-in-law, my mama and papa. My brother was born when I was almost seven, so I was the sole recipient of Pepère's kingly largesse for a long time.

"You spoil that boy too much!" my papa would say to my *pepère*.

"You don't spoil him enough!" Pepère would retort. And another round of that particular disagreement would begin. Since they disagreed about so many things—with varying levels of intensity—their arguments blended with the normal household sounds: the refrigerator door opening and closing, dishes clanking, or the tunes of the jigs and reels bouncing on the French radio station. They argued about local and national politics, about the unions in the mills, and even about the Boston Red Sox, though Papa seemed to care about the team only when he could give Pepère some grief about his "heroes who can't do a thing right."

There were, however, some areas of agreement. Sometimes, usually in the late evening after Mama or Papa had tucked me in to bed, I'd fall off to sleep to the muffled sounds of the three of them talking in the living room. My mother's presence may have affected the tone of these conversations, since they often turned to reminiscences about other times and other places—the relatives who still lived in Québec, the many trips to visit them, or the "big trip" that heads of families undertook crossing the border to work and live in the United States.

Thousands of people made that journey. They had to be ready to go when a better future beckoned. As a young boy, Pepére came across the border with his family. A generation later, his son-in-law, my papa, made the same journey. And they later moved their own families, in search of better jobs or better places, after they came to the States.

In those late evenings, the talk was warmer, though still animated. Then, usually after I was fast asleep, sometimes even after Mama had gone to sleep too, Pepère or Papa would say "Let's go for a ride!" and the other would invariably agree that it was a fine idea. Papa would wake Mama, who always liked to go for a ride, and she'd bundle me up for the trip as I continued sleeping. It was probably convenient for her at those moments that I was the kind of sleeper who would often fall out of bed, thump to the floor, be picked up and replaced in the bed by one of my parents, and never wake up.

Within minutes we'd be on our way—Papa driving, Pepère in the front seat, and Mama in the back with me cradled in her arms, my sleep undisturbed by the change of location.

We'd sometimes go for short trips, returning a few hours later. They'd lay me, still fast asleep, back in my bed, where the ride might seep through sleep crevices and into my dreams. But it wasn't unusual for the three to decide, after hitting the road, that it would be fun to surprise relatives in New Hampshire or Rhode Island by pulling into their driveways for a visit just as the sun was rising.

Doors swung open and a flurry of hearty and heartfelt *bonjours* and *allôs*, which "real" kings and their retinues could only wish for, were exchanged. And I would be tucked, dreams only slightly jostled, into yet another bed.

Within minutes, aunts, uncles, and cousins scurried around preparing breakfast while exchanging news and stories with Pepère, Mama, and Papa.

I'd later wake up to the sounds of the reunion and make my way to the kitchen for a breakfast of *crêpes*, sausages, *cretons* and *confitures* that were always fit for a king. We'd stay and visit; I'd play with cousins and friends; we'd say our goodbyes; and we'd be back home in time for my parents to carry my sleeping form to my bed.

Some of our ancestors had been sent to Canada by French kings to forge new lives in a harsh land. They had to be "ready to go" and leave their homeland in the first place, and "ready to go" after they arrived. Some of them had to be ready to clear forests or plant crops, others to travel up and down the wild rivers as hunters and trappers.

Maybe Pepère, Papa, and Mama still had that in their blood. And maybe they passed it on to me. They had been ready to go when they *had* to. And now they were also ready to go when they *wanted* to.

Pepère had often been forced by necessity and circumstance to be ready to go. When I knew him, he just *enjoyed* being ready to go. And that, more than anything, was what made Pepère a king.

Ti-Jean Dry Bread
Ti-Jean pain sec

✦✦✦✦✦✦✦✦✦✦✦✦✦✦✦✦

In this story the protagonist "picks up and goes" after his father kicks him out and sends him on his way with a paltry inheritance. So he goes to see what's over the next hill. Will he return? That will likely depend on what he finds.

"Ti-Jean, my son, I've taken care of you long enough. Pack your bags and get out!"

"Well, at least give me something to take with me," the son replied.

So his father gave Ti-Jean his inheritance—a loaf of bread, a bottle of milk, and five cents.

It was haying time and very hot. Ti-Jean was sweating and very tired of walking. He went into a meadow and sat under a tree. While he ate his bread and drank his milk, flies buzzed around him. "Flies, leave me in peace! When I'm finished, I'll give you something to eat," he said.

He broke off some bread crumbs, poured milk over them, and invited the flies to the feast. The flies covered the milky bread like a cloud. Ti-Jean smacked a thousand flies with one blow and five hundred with another. He then spent five cents to have a placard made that said, "Ti-Jean Dry-Bread killed a thousand with one blow and

23

five hundred with the next." Then, he lay down next to his sign and took a nap.

The king, who happened to be passing by, read Ti-Jean's placard. He said to his coachman, "Go ahead and wake him up!"

"Wake him up? So I can be killed!?"

"Wake him politely!"

The coachman approached. "My lord Ti-Jean, please wake up."

"What do you want?"

"His majesty the King would like to speak with you."

"Your majesty, what is it that you want?"

"Is it true, Sir Ti-Jean, that you killed a thousand with one blow and five hundred with the next?"

"On my word, it is true!" Ti-Jean replied.

"Do you want to render me service?"

"Yes, your majesty!"

"In my forest, there are three giants and a ferocious beast who ravage the countryside. Can you destroy them?"

"A ferocious beast?" Ti-Jean asked.

"Yes, a unicorn," the king said.

"And three giants?"

"The most terrible on earth."

"Your majesty, all that's needed is a flick of the wrist to flatten them all on the ground."

The king gave him food enough for a day, and Ti-Jean walked down the path toward the forest. And he walked. And he walked. He came upon a huge spruce tree around which were strewn piles of bones and garbage. "This must be where the giants eat their supper. I wonder what sort of brutes they are?" Ti-Jean asked himself. He picked up three stones and tucked them into his shirt. He climbed up the spruce tree and hid.

One of the giants arrived with a huge cherry tree on his back. He threw it—branches, dangling roots, and all—on the ground. The spruce tree shook as he did so. Ti-Jean said to himself, That's a fierce creature!

A second giant soon appeared with a barrel of water under each arm. And still a third brought a huge cooking pot and a dead bull that he threw on the ground—*Bing, Bang, Boom!*

They are truly monsters, Ti-Jean thought.

The first giant built an enormous crackling fire. The second dumped the water into the cooking pot and tossed the bull into it. The third stirred the boiling meat with a large wooden spoon. After they ate heartily, the giants stretched out beneath the tree and soon fell asleep.

Ti-Jean, clinging to a branch, threw one of his rocks at the mouth of the youngest giant, who was snoring. Bang! He broke one of the giant's teeth. He awoke in a fury and smacked the giant lying next to him. "That'll teach you to let me sleep in peace!" he said, and went right back to sleep.

Ti-Jean threw a larger rock at the second giant, breaking two of his teeth, then another one at the oldest giant, breaking three of his teeth. The giants woke up furious and started pounding each other.

They uprooted trees and smacked each other sense-less. They finally fell to the ground exhausted, barely breathing and barely conscious. Lucky for Ti-Jean, they'd fallen on their stomachs, their heads almost touching.

So he climbed down from the tree, pulled out his knife, and cut a thick lock of hair from each of the giants' shaggy heads. He used the hair to tie the giants' hands behind their backs. Then, he doomed the trio to final frustration and immobility by tying their three heads together in a series of tight knots, using thick ropes woven from their hair.

The king, upon seeing Ti-Jean return, cried out, "You're still alive, Ti-Jean!"

"Oh sure, youngsters like that, I took care of them with just a couple strokes."

"I can't believe it!" the king said.

"Come see for yourself then."

When the king saw the vanquished giants, he turned to Ti-Jean and said, "Ti-Jean, that is truly amazing. They should give us no more trouble. Now, in the depths of the forest lives a ferocious unicorn that is killing many of my people. Can you rid us of it?"

"I'll be glad to, but I'll need provisions."

"Whatever you want!" the king said. "This time follow the forest path to the very end."

Ti-Jean walked and walked and walked. And he thought, If I do see that evil beast, I'll have to run as fast as my legs will carry me.

Then, just as he approached an old abandoned church the unicorn appeared. Taken by surprise, Ti-Jean didn't have time to retreat. He ran for the church, and the beast pursued him. Quickly, Ti-Jean hid behind the door. As the unicorn thundered through the doorway, Ti-Jean darted out from behind the door, stepped out of the church, and closed the door, locking the beast inside.

The unicorn, eyes now bulging with fury, charged head-first into the walls that held it captive. Ti-Jean climbed to the bell tower, looked down at the unicorn, and rubbed his hands. "Go ahead, charge even harder!"

He returned to the castle. The king, upon seeing him, cried out, "Ti-Jean, it's you!"

"Yes, it's me! Who else?" Ti-Jean replied.

"How did you do it?"

"I caught it by the tail."

"I don't believe you."

"Come see for yourself, your majesty."

At the old church, Ti-Jean, with a wink of an eye, said, "I'm going to open the door."

"You watch yourself," the king said.

"I'm going to grab it by the tail."

"Oh no you don't! What if you miss!"

Quite content to avoid any added risks, Ti-Jean and the king climbed to the bell tower.

"Now we can always keep an eye on it," Ti-Jean said.

"Let's go, Ti-Jean! Better now to be thinking about our safety."

From that moment on, the king, Ti-Jean, and the people in the kingdom lived forever safe and happy.

Uncle Noël's Story

L'histoire de mon oncle Noël

Told to me by my Uncle Noël Boisvert in the mid-1970s, this is a family story about the migration days. It suggests that not all poor French-Canadian immigrants settled in mill towns or worked in the textile industry. Not at first, anyway. In Uncle Noël's story, the father bought a farm in Concord, New Hampshire, and supplemented the family income by working for the Water Works. When the older children eventually sought employment, the whole family moved to the closest textile city, in this case, Manchester. Family stories can often use a funny ending, and what is more incongruous than joking about a cemetery? Uncle Noël said ... (J.O.)

$\mathcal{M}$y father's family, the Boisverts, were from Saint-Thomas-de-Pierreville in the province of Québec. That's where my father, Alexandre Boisvert, was born on September 27, 1865, himself the son of Alexandre Boisvert.

Sometime after that date and before the turn of the century, Grandfather and Grandmother Boisvert left Canada for the United States. Their relatives and even their married children stayed in Canada. The Boisverts actually settled in Concord, the state capital—a twist since most Canadian settlers moved to industrial cities and worked in the textile mills. Or they settled in places like Berlin, working in the woods or in the paper industry.

But my grandparents came to Concord, a city with little or no industry. My grandfather got a job with the Water Works and worked for the city the rest of his life. He was well-respected and even became a foreman. Once established, my grandparents asked their children to join them in their adopted country. That's how my father and mother also left Québec and moved to Concord.

When they arrived in Concord, my parents already had three children—Victor, Hector, and Annie—all born during the 1890s. I was born on December 24, 1905, and my parents named me Alexandre after my father and grandfather. But they called me Noël. Like his father before him, my father got a job with the Water Works. These folks loved the land but missed farming. By skimping and saving, they finally bought a farm, the Larkin Farm, and well do I remember the place.

We had a big vegetable garden, and we kept cows. There was plenty of work to go around. And besides milking those cows and caring for them, we delivered the milk. So my father was also a milkman.

Meanwhile, the family grew. By 1908, Beatrice and Marie-Rose were added to the family. When I was four or five, my parents had to make a decision. You see, there wasn't much work available in Concord; so my older brothers wanted to head south to Manchester, where the Amoskeag Manufacturing Co. was becoming the biggest textile operation in the world. There were plenty of jobs in Manchester, and half the workers were French-Canadians. That's how the family decision came up. Would the oldest boys go off on their own, or would the whole family move to Manchester? Rather than break the family up, my parents decided we would all move.

The farm was sold, and a big auction was held for the household and farm items. We kept only the essentials: clothes, a little furniture, a few animals, and our horse and wagon. Then we left. What a day that was when our little caravan with parents and kids, horse and wagon headed south. Back then, eighteen miles was a whole day's journey, and I loved every minute of it, sitting up there on the wagon, going on the biggest adventure of my life.

Nobody wanted us—a big family in a strange city. My father went to the first apartment house, knocked on the door, and asked if there was a vacancy. The first question was: "Do you have any kids?"

"A few ..." my father answered.

When the owner heard we were a whole bunch, he said, "Sorry, there's no room."

We went to another tenement house. "Do you have an apartment?" my father asked.

"Maybe. You got kids?" was the man's question.

My father's answer brought another rejection. He tried elsewhere. Same question, same answer. "How many children? Sorry, there's no room."

Young as I was, even I realized we had a problem.

We were making our way toward the edge of town, a wooded area, in the direction of South Beech and Willow Streets, and it was getting late. By the time we got to the cemetery, the cimetière Saint-Augustin, my father had an idea. "You all stay here," he told us. He headed back a short distance to where more tenement houses sat. Again he knocked on the door and inquired about an apartment.

"Do you have any children?"

"Yes, sir, I do; but they are all in the cemetery!"

It worked.

Even when he found out he'd been tricked, the landlord let us stay. And we never spent much time in a cemetery after that.

The Split Boulder
Le Caillou coupé

✦✦✦✦✦✦✦✦✦✦✦✦✦✦✦✦✦✦

The French in North America trace their roots on the continent to the early sixteenth century travels of Giovanni da Verrazzano, who sailed for François I, King of France, and Jacques Cartier, the French explorer from Saint Malo. But legends and tales from the Norman coast as well as from the French islands of Saint Pierre et Miquelon off the southern coast of Newfoundland suggest a more ancient tradition, one of fishermen, adventurers, and souls lost at sea.

"The Split Boulder" is about those times before recorded history. It was written by an avid student of folklore and a well-known author from Saint Pierre. I enjoyed the story so much that it became a staple of my repertoire. In contacting the author, however, I learned that, much to my surprise, the tale was a product of her imagination. Why include it here then? Well, "The Split Boulder" is certainly in the tradition of explaining natural phenomena through stories; and, besides, legends have to begin somewhere, don't they? (J.O.)

*I*n the latter part of the seventh century, in the Norman seacoast town of Avranches, there lived a holy man named Aubert. Although he had already reached a respectable age, he had a young sister who was but fifteen. She was very beautiful and answered to the name Colombe, which means dove.

Brother and sister lived under the same roof, next door to the modest shop of Gildas, the wrought-iron artisan. Gildas, a quiet young man who usually kept his thoughts to himself, was madly in love with his comely neighbor; but, heaven having endowed him with a somewhat timid nature, he rarely spoke his feelings to anyone, least of all to Colombe.

One day in April, Colombe set off in a little boat to join her brother who was busy preaching in the south of England. The boat had practically reached port, and already the travelers could see the distant figures of those who awaited them on the shore when, suddenly, a violent storm erupted. A giant wave washed over the bridge and threw three of the crew into the sea leaving only Colombe and a young sailor who was on his maiden voyage.

The storm tossed the boat far from shore, and all through the day and night the two thought at least a thousand times they were about to die. By morning, however, the sea was nearly a total calm. The young sailor hoisted the sail and then fell fast asleep beside Colombe as the boat was rocked by the waves and pushed gently by a wind from the east.

For days and days, the two unfortunate beings bobbed about between heaven and earth. Hunger and thirst had drained them of three-quarters of their lives, so that they no longer had any hope of survival when a new storm arose, pushing the tiny craft far across the Atlantic Ocean and just to the south of what is now Newfoundland. Finally, on the southern tip of the island of Saint Pierre, their tiny craft was hurled against the rocks. In the shipwreck, the young sailor lost his life; but when she awoke, Colombe found herself on the beach, unscathed. She had washed up on what is called today Savoyard Cove.

Fortunately, Colombe was a person of untold resources. Moving inland and away from the wind and weather, she gathered branches and fabricated a shelter on the pond known as *le diamant*.

There she began her solitary existence, taking sustenance from the plants and fish. So it was, thanks to her instinctive abilities and extraordinary knowledge of nature's riches that she succeeded in surviving the long winter.

When spring came, Colombe roamed amid the flora, stooping occasionally to pick wild mint or to confide to some forget-me-not her hopes and dreams. Tender was the blue of the forget-me-nots, but more tender still was the heart of the young girl. On some nights, the modest flowers were incapable of chasing away the melancholy that welled up in Colombe. On those nights, the unfortunate castaway left the shores of the pond and spent long hours in the cove where her boat had broken apart. Longingly, she peered out to sea.

In the first weeks following the shipwreck, she had hoped that help might come from the large, mysterious island off in the distance. But no craft had ventured her way from the island's austere cliffs, and Colombe had ceased to scrutinize this land, apparently as deserted as her own. In Savoyard Cove, she now sought some sign of comfort, an illusion of human presence in the company of the earthly grave of the young sailor she herself had buried a long time ago.

Those who have witnessed on a splendid summer's evening a sunset at Savoyard Cove will understand that this scene had given Colombe the serenity that was most often hers. And, when night fell, she retraced her steps without a thought of sadness despite the fact that no one awaited her at the end of the path. Once again, she was reconciled, for a time, to her solitude.

Meanwhile, in Normandy, Gildas learned from Aubert that a storm had dragged Colombe out to sea. His love would not permit him to believe she had perished, or perhaps the intensity of that very love offered insight beyond the scope of human understanding. Gildas vowed to rescue his beloved. He knew no rest until he, too, had found a ship to seek out the one he considered his fiancée. When once again he would gaze upon her, he would not hesitate to make known his love.

So it was that Gildas sailed from Normandy. Year after year he combed the seas without ever finding the island of Saint Pierre. For thirty-two years, he searched in vain, and for thirty-two years, Colombe looked in vain to the East for the ship that would take her back to her native land.

In the thirty-third year, Gildas returned home to learn that his neighbor, the holy and saintly Aubert, had been named bishop of Avranches and that he had built a shrine on *Mont-Tombe*. Gildas decided that the rugged and desolate rock, sometimes beaten by the waves, at other times surrounded by moving sands, was a ready-made refuge for his wounded heart. He went to the holy place to live out his remaining years.

It was in this hermitage that, after several decades given to prayer and meditation, Gildas died. One grey November night, his spirit floated to paradise. During his life, Gildas had learned the hard way the difficulty of relying on one's own human abilities to find a loved one lost somewhere in this vast world. Free of his body, he now saw the chance to use supernatural means to communicate with his soul mate. It seemed to him that the simplest method—and certainly the best known—was to appear to her in a dream.

But either through lack of experience or because the circumstances were not right, Gildas was not immediately able to break into his beloved's dreams. Being a persevering soul, however, he did not let that discourage him; and thus he was rewarded. One fine spring afternoon, as Colombe rested in the shade of a pine tree, their two spirits met in sleep.

In order to show the depth and breadth of his feelings, Gildas recounted his exhaustive search of the seas and his long years of existence on the stone hill of Mont-Tombe. Then, with great eloquence, he begged Colombe to come join him. Sadly, Gildas neglected one detail—telling his beloved exactly where he was.

Colombe awoke overwhelmed by the revelation of this unknown love, and she was at first filled with regret for the loss that had been her life. Then she began to think: Was this dream perhaps something more than a passionate declaration of love? Was there not in it a message of some sort, an urgent cry to go somewhere?

Filled with this thought, Colombe put all her energy into remembering—before they floated away completely—the words of her lover. Alas! Despite her best efforts, certain words succeeded in drifting away. Others got quite muddled to the point where it was difficult to understand their meanings.

Poor Colombe's long isolation had somewhat clouded her mind, and her memory sometimes played tricks on her. Nevertheless, she stuck to her task, and little by little she reconstructed the message—or rather what she thought to be the message—of Gildas. Where was she to go? She remembered that he had spoken of a rock ... so Colombe came to believe her beloved had set up a rendezvous at some rock or boulder. But which one?

Ah! She concluded that rock of rendezvous could be none other than the large boulder by her pond. There on the hill, to the far side of the water, the boulder stood like a hut among the pines. And from that moment, the unhappy Colombe, convinced that she now knew what Gildas expected of her, spent practically all her time at the foot of the boulder, patiently awaiting the arrival of her love.

But no one came. Even in dream, the fiancé never reappeared, and her hope ebbed like the tide.

One night, as Colombe waited, sitting on the rock in what had become her habitual spot and remembering the days when she lived in Normandy next door to Gildas, she began thinking about her brother, Aubert. He was already old when she had seen him last. Without doubt, he must now be in paradise, for she remembered him as a saintly man. In her sadness, she conceived the idea of invoking his aid. Climbing atop the boulder to be closer to heaven, Colombe addressed this fervent prayer.

"Aubert, my dear brother," she said, "I pray to you. Please come to my help! All my life I hoped in vain to escape this solitude that surrounds me. And now, today, when I have found the love of a fine boy, this companion tarries so in joining me that I fear he has lost his way. Please help us find one another because I feel myself getting older by the day. And each moment the pain of exile weighs more heavily upon my weary heart."

This moving prayer was heard by the old bishop of Avranches who was now, as his sister had suspected, in paradise. In fact, he enjoyed both a new status and a fine reputation because he had become Saint Aubert, which gave to his supplications a certain added value. For that reason, Aubert felt confident in going to find God the Father to pray for the reunion of Colombe and Gildas. The request was deemed reasonable by the Creator who at once sent a formidable thunderstorm over the island of Saint-Pierre, with lightning dubbed *le chalin* by later residents.

Without warning, lightening dazzled the sky, and one fierce bolt instantly hit Colombe. In that light and during the rolling of the thunder, her soul entered paradise and was united with Gildas, who had so long awaited her. The celestial power also split the grey boulder on which Colombe had prayed. It is said that angels gently bore her body to the earth between the two giant pieces.

Some say that God later took Gildas's body from the stone at Mont-Saint-Michel and miraculously transported it to the grey rock that enfolded the earthly remains of Colombe.

If you make your way to the pond just up the road from Savoyard Cove, you can still see the boulder that people call *le caillou coupé*. It was split in two one day by the grace of a brother's fervent prayer, uniting for all eternity Colombe, the solitary castaway, with Gildas, the persevering lover.

Ti-Jean Joins the Elite
Ti-Jean et l'élite

The classic choices—"Grow where you're planted" versus "Go find out what's over the next hill." If the choice boils down to the struggle of maintaining a meager existence among the people where you are known and feel at home, or following the urge to seek fortune among strangers, there are those who choose one or the other, and those who try both before making their choice.

a long time ago, Ti-Jean lived with his mama and worked for the lord of the manor, just as his dear departed papa had done. One day, when he and his neighbors were tilling the fields, the lord rode by in his gilded carriage, and one of Ti-Jean's fellow workers muttered, "Peacock on wheels!"

After the lord had passed, Ti-Jean leaned on his hoe, looked toward the huge estate, and said, "Someday I will have a carriage like that, I too will live in a fine, stone house, and I will be part of the elite." This announcement was greeted by howls of ridicule from his friends and neighbors, but Ti-Jean paid no attention. He had decided to become a member of the elite.

That evening at supper he asked his mama, "How does a person become part of the elite, Mama?"

"Well, my son, most are born into it."

"Does a person have to be very smart?"

"No, no," she said, "many of them are fools."

"But suppose a person is not born into the elite. Are there other ways to do it, Mama?"

"Oh yes," she said, "there are ways. But it's not easy."

"Tell me, Mama, what are those ways?"

"Well, one could become a lawyer."

"Oh yes, Mama, they are certainly part of the elite. But how does one go about becoming a lawyer?"

"You should practice, practice, practice for weeks and months on end. You should ..."

"Practice what, Mama? Tell me please."

"Lying."

"What is that you say, Mama?"

"You must practice lying to become a lawyer, because when you become one, you must stand up in a large room—a court room— and tell a lie. Then, your opponent will take his turn and try to tell a bigger lie. And you will go back and forth telling lies until another fool, called the judge, decides which one of you has lied the best."

"Oh, Mama," Ti-Jean said somberly, "I don't think that is how I can become a member of the elite. You know very well that I am not a skilled liar. I've never been able to fool you or anybody else with any lie I've ever told."

"Well then, maybe you could try to become a doctor."

"A doctor? What a wonderful idea! How would I go about becoming a doctor, Mama?"

"First, you must collect plants and herbs and flowers and weeds for making potions. Then you must learn a lot of big words that nobody will understand ..."

"Must I also learn their meanings, Mama?"

"Not necessarily. But most important, my dear Ti-Jean, is that you must have confidence, and the gift to make sick people feel that they are getting better."

"Is there anything else required, Mama?"

"No, I don't think so my son."

"Then, I will become a doctor, and in that way become a member of the elite!"

"May God go with you, my son. And remember where it is that you are both known and loved."

Ti-Jean couldn't wait to get started. The very next day, he took to the roads and byways. As he walked along, he collected the herbs, plants, weeds, and flowers needed for his potions. He created and tasted various concoctions as he traveled from village to village looking for sick people to cure. And he, of course, listened for and learned as many large words as he could.

But he sadly discovered that, in one place after another, there was no interest in his services. Walking into the center of a town or a village, he'd announce himself confidently—*"Bonjour*, I am Ti-Jean, the world's greatest doctor! I'm here to cure the sick among you!"—and be completely ignored.

Finally, after many such attempts, an old villager told Ti-Jean that there really was no need for his skills there since they had a local curing lady who took care of such things. "But I can tell you," the old man continued, "that the king whose castle lies a three-day walk to the west of here has many sick people needing to be cured. But he can be a harsh man, so don't make any promises you can't keep."

Ti-Jean thanked the old man and set out. He traveled through the forest, over the mountain, and into the valley until he arrived at the king's castle.

He knocked at the great oaken castle door. When it swung open, he announced himself to the guard. "Hello, I am Ti-Jean, the world's greatest doctor! I am here to cure the sick people in this castle!" The guard sneered and closed the door in Ti-Jean's face. But Ti-Jean remembered Mama's words about confidence and knocked again. The guard again opened the door, listened to the same announcement, grabbed Ti-Jean, and flung him down the castle steps.

The king overheard the commotion and summoned the guard. "What, pray tell, is going on at the gate?" he asked.

"Your majesty, it's a ridiculous bumpkin announcing himself as the world's greatest doctor. But I've gotten rid of him."

The king considered this for a moment. "The world's greatest doctor? Well, this could at least be entertaining. Bring him in!"

When Ti-Jean was brought before the king, he again boldly proclaimed, "Good day and good health to you, your majesty! I am Ti-Jean, the world's greatest doctor! I am here to cure the sick people in this castle!"

"And what proof do you offer," the king said, "that you are, indeed, what you say you are?"

"Well, your majesty, do you have any ailments yourself that I might suggest a cure for?"

"Oh, let's see," the king said. "Yes, actually I do. My stomach has been upset lately when I eat the meat of the caribou. What would you prescribe for that?"

Without hesitation, Ti-Jean replied, "Your majesty, for that ailment I would recommend that you take an infusion of a fomentation made from the purple herb that grows on the shady side of the lost mountain in the misty forest."

The king whispered to his most trusted advisor. "This man is very clever. Did you hear the words he used? The peasant costume must simply be a disguise." Then he turned to Ti-Jean. "And so Monsieur the Doctor, how do you propose to cure the sick people in my castle?"

"My dear benevolent majesty, surely you are keenly aware that there are spies everywhere who would like nothing better than to steal my secrets. I can only tell you that, when I am finished, all the sick people will feel much better, and you will see this for yourself."

"Oh yes? Well then, how shall we proceed? And what shall you demand as reward if you are successful?"

"Your majesty," Ti-Jean solemnly replied, "though I am a great doctor, I am yet a simple man. So if you could manage it, I would like, as my reward, half the lands in your kingdom, your daughter's hand in marriage, five cooking pots filled with gold coins, and a fine carriage with a team of six shiny black horses."

"Those are the conditions of a confident man," the king said. "And I will accept them, if you can accept that I will have you beheaded if you fail."

"That will be fine, your majesty, and here is what is required for the cure. First, I'll need a room large enough to hold all the sick. In that room, I must have a roaring fire under a cauldron filled with water. This cauldron must be large enough for me to stand in. Finally, your majesty, I must have your royal pledge that you will not question any of the cured people about the secret means by which they were healed of their ailments."

The king commanded that Ti-Jean's orders be carried out. Soon all the sick were gathered in a room where they watched as Ti-Jean slowly stoked the fire and stirred the water in the cauldron. When all was ready, Ti-Jean signaled for the door to be closed and spoke to the group. "Dear people, I am Ti-Jean, the world's greatest doctor. I must tell you first that you must not reveal the means of your cure—the king himself has pledged not to question any of you—because it is well known that such a revelation will make you sicker than you've ever been in your life."

The sick and infirm looked at Ti-Jean with hopeful eyes. "And so the first thing I must do," he continued, "is to find out which one of you is the sickest person in this room." His eyes slowly scanned their faces. He moved around the room looking into their eyes. "When I do find that person, we will have the beginning of all your cures. Because when that person steps forward, we will boil him in the cauldron to make a healing potion." He paused again. "Then you will all drink from that potion and be cured."

None of the sick blinked even an eyelash as Ti-Jean walked around the room. When he returned to the cauldron to stoke the fire and wait for someone to step forward, the door opened, and a dozen people slipped out and sauntered gaily into the castle courtyard, feeling better than they had in years. Ti-Jean then approached one sick person, and another, inquiring if he or she might be the sickest person in the room. One man, grabbing his crutches, said, "Monsieur the Doctor, I am cured just looking into your eyes!" and ran out into the hallway.

One after another, they made their exits until, after just one hour, no sick people were left in the room.

The king saw people skipping lightly down the hallways. A servant informed him that the room was indeed cleared of the sick. So he was satisfied that they all felt much better. Within hours, arrangements were made for Ti-Jean's wedding to the princess. The king gave Ti-Jean half the royal lands, outfitted a fine carriage with six shiny black horses for him, and had the five cooking pots full of gold coins delivered to Ti-Jean's new chambers in the castle.

"It worked," Ti-Jean said as he ran his hands through the gold coins. "I am now a member of the elite. Mama was right!"

Within days, Ti-Jean was spending his gold coins furiously, riding through the kingdom in his carriage, attending lavish parties with and without the princess, and generally living the grand life.

Within weeks, however, he had spent the gold, used up the princess' patience, and begun to sell off parcels of the royal lands to continue living the life of the elite.

Within months, Ti-Jean had squandered everything, including any affection the princess had for him, had run his fine carriage and shiny black horses into the ground, and been banished from the castle by the king.

What could Ti-Jean, world's greatest doctor, do now?

He considered many grand schemes and glittering possibilities as he stumbled along the roads, his dreams shattered. He soon made a decision. Within a few days, Ti-Jean arrived at Mama's door.

She welcomed him with open arms, fed him well, and listened to his story. "I suppose, Mama," he said finally, "you have reason to be proud of how cleverly I was able to join that great club—the elite. But as you can see, I did not do very well as an actual member of that club."

To which Mama replied, "You're still a fine young man, Ti-Jean. And now you know the difference between a club and a home. Have a good sleep, my son. Tomorrow will be a new day."

My Grandfather the Magician
Mon grand-père le magicien

✤✤✤✤✤✤✤✤✤✤✤✤✤✤✤✤✤

This is a story about my maternal grandfather, Alexis Lacasse. As the oldest daughter and the third of twelve children, my mother, Alice Lacasse Olivier, remembered many stories about those days in the Amoskeag Mills and the corporation housing in Manchester, New Hampshire. During the depression, only radio and an occasional movie existed as entertainment—especially for poor mill workers. Harry Houdini had captured the country's imagination because magicians offered a chance to escape the harsh realities of everyday life. As a storyteller, my grandfather felt free to borrow from Houdini's fame. (J.O.)

*B*orn in Magog, Québec, in 1890, Alexis Lacasse was the youngest of fifteen children. At age fifteen, he migrated to the United States, and five years later he married Maria Grenier of Trois-Rivières. Despite his lack of a formal education, Alexis became a loom-fixer and eventually made lower-level management as a "second-hand."

Status has its privileges, and in those days perks were cheap. My grandfather possessed the key to the cupola in No. 3 Mill, where each noon he took refuge from the dust and incessant clanging of the looms to eat a relatively quiet lunch and read the local French newspaper, *L'Avenir National*.

After the death of their first child, Alexis and Maria became parents of twelve healthy children. My mother was the third, and Lionel was the eighth. This story is about Lionel.

Everyone called him Nénel; they did that, in fact, until his death in the late 1980s when he was well into his sixties. Nénel was everyone's favorite, a thin, fair-haired child, who was always smiling. Every noon, Nénel's job was to take his father's lunch to the storage room in the mill cupola. This was no sandwich-and-box-cookie deal; this was a whole *dîner*, as people called the noon meal in those days, complete with meat and potatoes on china dishes. Nénel stayed until his papa finished, and then he returned home with the dishes.

Now, Alexis was quite a storyteller. Sometimes, he told tales from the old days in Canada. Sometimes, he just created them. That's how, one day, he happened to tell his children that he was a magician like Houdini.

"In fact," he boasted, "you know that room where I have lunch? Well, even if the door was locked, I could get out!"

The older ones smiled and took his claim of supernatural powers with a grain of salt. Nénel did not. If Papa said it, then it had to be true!

One day, Nénel decided to give his papa the opportunity to show his magic. Wasting no time after he was no longer needed, Nénel said nothing, took the dishes, and walked out. Closing the door, he turned the big key in the lock before leaving the cupola. There was too much noise for his father to hear the key turn, but Nénel knew Papa would be fine.

Nénel crossed the canal and Canal Street, reaching his corporation home on Market Street within a few minutes.

He put the dishes into the sink and told his mother, "Papa's going to do his trick." Nénel was never one to hide the truth. Besides, he really had nothing to worry about and no reason to feel guilty.

Mama thought the preschooler was kidding and paid no attention to him.

Alexis had been surprised at Nenel's rapid departure but hadn't thought any more about it. Having finished his lunch, he went to the door and was astonished to find it locked. He shouted for help until he was hoarse. But no one heard him. The looms were just too loud. So Alexis, the second-hand, spent the whole afternoon in the cupola. What would he ever tell the workers ... and his boss? Maybe later, after everyone was gone, he could get through the window without being seen. The afternoon dragged on. At exactly six o'clock, the big bell in the tower signaled the end of the twelve-hour work day. Thousands of men and women filed out of the mills, which snaked for one mile along the Merrimack River.

Soon the workers were gone, and Alexis made his move. He tried the window. It wouldn't open. So he broke the pane and stepped out onto the roof.

Down in the employment office, someone looked up and spotted a man on the roof of the cupola. "What in the devil is he doing up there?" The office called Mr. Cramm, the boss in No. 3 Mill.

"What's happened in your mill? There's a man on the roof!"

Mr. Cramm went up and unlocked the door. He looked around the storage room, but no one was there. Only a broken window.

In the meantime, Alexis was on his way home in his work clothes. In those days, people never left the mill dirty; they always washed and changed into their good clothes. That day, though, Alexis had no choice but to go home the way he was.

The family always ate by six-fifteen. That's the way it was every day. But not this day. Where was Papa? Only Nénel didn't seem worried. Contrary to all custom, Maria decided to say the prayer and start the meal without her husband.

"*Au nom du Père et du Fils et du Saint-Esprit.*" (In the name of the Father and of the Son and of the Holy Spirit.)

"*Ainsi soit-il.*" (Amen.)

"*Bénissez-nous Seigneur ainsi que la nourriture....*" (Bless us, O Lord, and these thy gifts....)

And they began to eat without Papa.

They'd only taken a few bites when the door swung open and banged against the wall. Alexis nearly tore off the knob. Normally a gentle man, he had quite a temper when he got mad. When the children were at fault, he got his big razor strap to set things straight.

"Where is he?" he yelled. "Get me my strap!"

"Oh no you don't!" the usually quiet Maria said. No one was going to do her Nénel in. "You called this on yourself. I told you that you shouldn't tell such stories to the children. It's your own fault."

The only one who thought this episode was funny was Mr. Cramm. He was a jovial man, and he laughed when he found out what had happened.

Alexis never punished Nénel. And he never again bragged about being a magician.

The Other World

L'Autre Monde *was often populated by the good and evil spirits associated with Catholic beliefs. For example, the Devil occasionally showed up when people crossed an imaginary behavioral-religious line drawn by priests and the Church. But at times, monsters such as the* loup-garou *appeared from the Other World and reinforced those same beliefs, providing the spiritual or psychic restraints necessary to curb irreligious, immoral, or even unconventional behavior. It was sometimes said, for instance, that someone who had not fulfilled basic religious obligations would become a* loup-garou, *as was the case for Hubert, the miller's helper in* "The Loup-Garou." *Countless tales also exist about saints, the Blessed Virgin Mary, Jesus, and God the Father providing various kinds of help to believers in need. The* lutins—*elf-like creatures who sometimes played exasperating jokes on farmers—though perhaps not directly connected to people's religious beliefs, seemed to also indicate that French-Canadians of yesteryear, like people in general, often saw the world as a mysterious place where amazing things could happen.*

The Handsome Dancer
Le beau danseur

✠✦✠✦✠✦✠✦✠✦✠✦✠✦✠✦✠

In a physically and emotionally daunting environment where it was more often cold and dark than warm and light, the reassurance of clearly drawn moral and spiritual lines served as a buffer against the unknown and the forces of evil. It was a world of moral "blacks and whites" and very few grays. The Catholic Church and its priests were the guides and protectors of "the faithful" against "the forces of darkness," which often used worldly pleasures —like dancing—to lead the faithful into temptation. And they were, indeed, strict guides. One misstep, as José Moreau learns, can have serious consequences.

G reat rejoicing filled José Moreau's house that Saturday night. His son, Pierre, had returned after a three-year stay in the United States. José had killed the fatted calf to celebrate the arrival of his prodigal son.

After supper the chairs and benches were lined against the walls, although dancing was not planned since such liberties were not taken in this house. Better parishioners than José and his family couldn't be found in all of Lislet. They were good, upright people. José was the very model of an honest man, humble, generous, and as straight as the king's own spear. He knew very well that the Church forbade dancing. José certainly didn't want to fall into disgrace.

But it was only fitting to rejoice heartily upon the return of Pierre, their eldest and his mother's favorite son. That's why rum and curaçao sat on the table and, even better, some contraband liquor from the islands of Saint-Pierre and Miquelon. Such spirits had never been seen at José and Catherine Moreau's house, but one occasion does not create a custom.

José felt a bit uneasy, however, when a group of young people he barely knew came in after supper. He feared some troublemakers had made their way into the party. They arrived with Dédé, the fiddler from down the road. Dédé of the wild feet and nimble tongue. But José, a polite, accommodating fellow, suppressed his annoyance. After all, wasn't Dédé a childhood pal of Pierre, like the other nice young men here? So José said, "Welcome all, and make yourselves at home."

In an instant, Dédé, tapping his feet, riding the bow on his fiddle strings, and "dropping the reins," as they used to say when the music galloped free, hollered, "*Allons-y!*"

"What do you call that tune?" asked François, one of Dédé's cohorts. "

"That happens to be *The Devil's Dream*, my friend," Dédé replied. And he jumped to another familiar tune, as though to throw François off track.

"And this one?" François asked.

"That's *The Wildcard*," Dédé said. "It comes from the Irish at Saint Malachi who sleep all day and dance all night." Turning to the group gathered around him, he asked, "Do you know the Saint Malachi Irish?"

"The Irish? Don't know them!" his lackeys—who hadn't traveled nearly as much as Dédé—replied.

"Listen, you people," Dédé said. "My friend Ruel and I were staying at the hotel in Saint-Malachi when the hostess said, 'Come with us tonight to an Irish wedding.' So we went. The house was full of people, Irish men and women. When the time for dancing came, there were a half-dozen bottles of all kinds on the table. My friend, Ruel, likes the booze, always has. He was offered a drink and gladly accepted. As for me, I didn't want any. Temperance, my friends."

Gales of incredulous laughter interrupted Dédé while François, getting the message, poured him a glass of white whisky. He downed it in one gulp and continued his story. "Ruel, seeing those tall Irishmen and all those bottles, said, 'Dédé, if these guys get fired up with all that liquor and lose their heads, they'll kill us both, for sure!' I tried to calm him. 'Don't worry about it. If anyone loses his head, it'll likely be you!'

"Just then the dancing began. The fiddler asked me to lead the dance with him, to trade tune for tune. I played one called *The Growling Woman*, and he played *The Wildcard*, a whale of a good dance tune—zing, zing. My pal Ruel, curious as ever, slipped in and said, 'What do you think? We don't even know the bride. Have you seen her? No? Well, shouldn't we introduce ourselves?'

"'Come on,' I replied, 'She's in her mother and father's bedroom.' We walked in and found a young woman asleep in an easy chair, nursing a child. She was blonde and full-figured, as beautiful as a dream. Ruel was beside himself. He hadn't often seen anything like this. 'Relax, my friend,' I said, 'Don't make a big deal about such things. That doesn't mean that they aren't good and fine people.'

"'But,' Ruel said, 'What I don't understand is that this young bride has a year-old child at her own wedding.' So I explained the whole thing to him."

"The whole thing? What on earth are you talking about, old pal?" the incredulous François exclaimed.

"Well, here's how it works," Dédé continued. "When an Irish couple marries in the summer, it's the custom to move the wedding party to a time after the fall harvest. But these people's house burned down, and they had to push the party back until the next year. So that's why Ruel and I saw the bride with her year-old child on her lap."

Finally understanding the puzzle, the people at José Moreau's cried in full voice, "Long live the bride at Saint Malachi! She fulfilled *all* her obligations—religious and otherwise—promptly and well!"

Dédé, tapping his feet with renewed vigor, started playing *The Wildcard*. This Irish dance tune hopped with such life that the chairs around the room started swaying.

What a pity to waste such lively music!

François, overcome by the music, walked to the sitting room and pleaded with José, the master of the house.

"Would you please start the dancing?"

"Start the dancing?" Now, José was embarrassed. He turned to Catherine.

"Should we ... shall we dance?"

"Why not?" Catherine smiled, good-natured as she was stout. "It's not every day that our Pierre returns after such a long absence."

José rose, extended his arm to Catherine, and they danced the first steps and not at all badly. They had certainly known how to have a good time in their younger days. And now their youth returned to them. In an instant, people crowded the dance floor.

The great Dédé, wound up and ready to go for twenty-four hours, kept the beat with his heel, worked his bow, and could have made the dust fly, had there been any dust in Catherine's house.

Between dances, liquid spirits were sampled and the dancers' spirits became enlivened. Soon, the merrymakers turned to singing, telling stories, and other amusements. Catherine, after holding her sides from laughing, was suddenly very moved by a sad song one of the uninvited rustics was singing. He had clumsily injected a note of melancholy into the rollicking fun. Everyone became silent. Then, a tinkling of bells came to their ears from outside the house, followed by the sound of a carriage slicing through the frozen snow.

"Whoa! Stop! Whoa!" a voice from outside commanded.

The clock struck eleven as three knocks sounded at the door.

"Come in! " José said.

The door opened. A stranger appeared on the doorstep, a young man with curly hair and a long, silky beard that was as black as crow feathers. His eyes flashed with a dark glimmer. The man, well-dressed, wore a beaverskin coat, a cap of velvety marten, and caribou moccasins embroidered with porcupine quills and pearls the shades of the rainbow.

The man walked in and gracefully greeted the gathering. He threw his coat and hat into a corner but didn't remove his black deerskin gloves. The young men thought he was putting on airs like a dandy from the city. The girls on the dance floor, however, could see no other partner from that moment on. He gazed at them with admiring, almost lustful, eyes. All the girls could see was an absolute gentleman with fine manners.

The stranger looked around, and his eyes settled on Pierre's sister, Blanche—the young lady of the house and the loveliest girl in the region. She had light skin, as her name suggested, finely sculpted features, and a lovely figure. She was not only pretty and comely but was known

as a real lady, sparkling with spirit, and the heart-throb of
the young men of Lislet.

She blushed all the way into the whites of her eyes
when the handsome stranger asked her to dance. Everyone watched her, and she felt completely clumsy and
embarrassed. Far from being at ease, she was hesitant and
began trembling inside.

"My, you are lovely," her dance partner whispered.

"Sir, I barely know how to dance," she replied. "Please
forgive me!"

The sweet hypocrite! There was no better dancer in all
of Lislet, and she knew it.

Some of the party-goers went outside to admire the
handsome dancer's carriage. It gleamed like a mirror and
was full of buffalo skins lined with red felt. And what a
horse! His eyes were so alert that he seemed almost human
and capable of speech. He must have come from far away,
maybe from the United States, a powerful race horse with
legs like iron, a fine, chiseled head, quivering nostrils, and
eyes like flames in the shadows—a true champion. The
horse traders had never seen his equal. He was covered
with frost, so he must have traveled far. Silver buckles
adorned his brand new, all-white harness of polished
leather. François went in to ask the horse's master if he'd
like the horse unharnessed, taken to the stable, and fed
some oats.

"Don't bother," the stranger replied curtly. "Just
throw one of the skins from the carriage on him. That'll be
sufficient. I only stopped because I noticed the party and
thought I might come in and dance two or three steps."

And what a dancer! François couldn't get over it. He
watched with his mouth agape, and it wasn't as though he
didn't know his dancers. "My, my, what a dancer!" he
repeated. "I've never seen anyone as good. There's no way

to explain all those steps he makes. He surely invents them as he goes along."

The stranger danced a straight jig that lasted at least a half-hour. He seemed tireless. The best dancers tried in vain to keep up with him, but one after another retreated to their seats. And he just kept going. Some of the young wise guys tried to show him up but soon realized they were dealing with a master. He simply threw them a glance, turned still another fancy step, and that was enough. Each of the youngsters withdrew sheepishly to his seat. Then the stranger improvised pirouettes, half-flying through the air as he executed them.

Finally, as a master-stroke, he decided to challenge Dédé. When the fiddler realized this, he thought it a rude maneuver, but his own vanity compelled him to accept the challenge. Blinded with sweat and fired by rage, he played on.

Crack! A fiddle string snapped. Had he broken it on purpose to catch his breath? In any event, the replacement time allowed him to compose himself. One of the dancers took the opportunity to organize a *cotillon*. Would the stranger take the lead? Without wasting even a moment, the handsome dancer stepped up, flashed a smile at one of the girls, said a flattering word to another, and winked at still another.

With another glass of Jamaican rum under his belt, Dédé was ready to go with renewed energy. Fiddle perched on his shoulder, he seemed as fresh as he had at the beginning. "Everyone forward. Dancers ready!" François cried in his clear song leader's voice. "Take your places for the *cotillon!*"

The dancing began, and the stamping of feet woke up little Paul, the two-year old, in his cradle. Catherine picked him up and sat watching from the bedroom door. But the child covered his face whenever the stranger danced near.

"Bur ... Bur ... Bur ... the man ...!" he stammered. "The man burns!" and he burst into tears. The handsome dancer gazed furiously at the child, as though he wanted to destroy him.

I wonder why the baby is so unsociable tonight? Catherine thought.

The girl who was dancing with the stranger wore a lovely necklace adorned with a crucifix. When she and the stranger came spinning past, Catherine heard him say to the girl, "Would you like to exchange that neck piece for this locket? It has my picture in a diamond setting!"

Catherine was suddenly jolted by an eerie foreboding.

She instantly rose from her chair. Carrying her youngest child in her left arm, Catherine went into the bedroom. She dipped her trembling fingers into the holy water basin at the head of the bed. Then, she walked straight to the stranger and made the sign of the cross in his direction.

The Devil—yes, for that is who he was—howled and leapt to the ceiling. He streaked toward the outside door, but the black cross of *le lacondaire*, the Temperance League, on the wall stopped him cold. Crazed with rage, he turned left and threw himself against the house's stone wall, breaking through with one blow. The house withstood the rupture but trembled on its foundation. Amidst the clanging of chains, the stranger flew to his carriage. A trail of sparks flashed from his horse's hooves as the carriage bolted into the night. An odious stench hung in the air.

Regaining their senses, the stunned gathering examined the gaping hole in the wall and the area outside the house. The snow had melted for one hundred yards around. Through the gloomy night, they all hurried back to their homes. José Moreau remained troubled and inconsolable. Why should he be the one to fall victim to such a disaster— he who had avoided scandal all his life?

The next day, the stonemason tried to repair the wall but absolutely could not. As soon as he put a stone in place, it shot off like a cannonball. Nothing could fill up the hole. The parish priest came and blessed the house. The saintly man spread his benedictions and left without a word to the disgraced José.

The breach in the wall could never be repaired, and the old stone house still sits abandoned in the middle of the uncultivated field.

The *Loup-Garou*
Le loup-garou

The loup-garou *is described in various ways—a wolf-like creature, a large wild dog, and even a werewolf. I've also heard it
described (by my Uncle Ray, for instance) as something closer
to a wolverine. But the* loup-garou *is almost always depicted
as a man who becomes a wild animal, usually because of a moral
or religious transgression. (M.P.)*

*I*n the North woods, the deep solitude and the plain-
tive cries of the cold wind as it blows through the pine
and fir trees touch human life with an added air of
mystery and, sometimes, darkness and shadow.

Many old people in the village of Beauséjour remember the name Joachim Crête, who was once the miller
there. He fasted during Lent and did not eat meat on
Fridays. But he ridiculed the collection of donations given
to the church during mass, gave no money in tithe to the
pastor, and employed a nonreligious man named Hubert
Savageau, under the pretext that Hubert was a good
checkers player.

So it was on one Christmas Eve, Joachim and Hubert
played checkers as they drank their fill of whisky, while
everyone else in the parish prepared for midnight mass.
As his neighbors walked to church, they called out to the

men. The checker players replied by jeering the churchgoers while continuing their party. They even opened the sluice-gates to start the mill wheels turning as the sound of the church bells echoed, slightly muffled by the blanket of snow covering the ground. Joachim felt a moment of shame, briefly, as he remembered his youth and his parents, but the game and drink pulled him away from such thoughts.

Suddenly, as the bell sounded its last tintinnabulations, the noise of the mill wheel stopped, and all was silent. The two men arose to start the wheel rolling again, but it seemed that a stronger hand resisted their efforts.

"To hell with it," Joachim said. "Let's get out of here!" Fear was quickly gaining the upper hand and with good reason. At that same moment, Joachim's lantern flickered out. Hubert then took a few steps in the dark, tripped and crashed down the stairs.

Joachim made his way to the empty table, where he relighted the lantern and tried to get a quick shot of courage from the half-empty bottle. Hearing the sound of light footsteps, he stood, turned, and screamed in terror. A huge, black, wolflike animal, eyes glowing, moved toward him, flashing long, sharp teeth.

"Hubert, help!" Joachim cried, but the beast was already crouching to leap at him.

Just then, the church bells rang again for the elevation, a solemn moment in the mass. Joachim fell to his knees. "Forgive me, O God! Save me from the loup-garou!" A large iron hook hung near the door. Joachim grabbed it, struck the beast and fell to the floor, exhausted and unconscious.

A while later, Joachim came to when Hubert threw water in his face. He looked up at his employee and checkers partner. "Your ear is bleeding, Hubert. What happened?"

"Oh, it's nothing," Hubert said, embarrassed and avoiding Joachim's eyes. "I scratched myself a couple days ago and must have reopened the gash when I fell."

Joachim looked at his companion more closely and considered the frightful turn of the evening's events. "Oh, you wretched man," Joachim cried in horror, "it was you!"

The miller fell backwards, howling madly; and they say he was "never quite right" after that.

The *Lutin* and the Hay Wagon
Le lutin et la carriole

✣✳✣✳✣✳✣✳✣✳✣✳✣✳✣✳✣

This story can fall into the category of either myth or legend. It attempts to explain a phenomenon, which the Catholic Church either did not explain, ignored as trivial, and/or dismissed as superstition.

Once there was a man, and so many *lutins* lived at his farm that he was at his wits' end. The man kept his hay wagon in the middle of the barn. Whenever he went into the barn late at night though, he discovered that his wagon was gone. The *lutins*, it seemed, had harnessed his horse to it and taken off.

In the morning, the horse's mane was always braided, a sure sign—some people said—that the animal had been used by *lutins*. Some of his friends and neighbors told him not to be concerned, since it was well-known that the *lutins*, though they rode the horses hard, always took very good care of the animals once the ride was finished. Certain horses, they said, even grew fatter and healthier in the *lutins'* care.

Other people, of course, said just the opposite.

One day, he said to himself, I'm going to find out once and for all if it is indeed the *lutins* who are taking my horse and wagon during the night. So he went out to the barn and hid in the wagon, slipping under some coverings he'd found.

Around midnight, the barn doors opened. In no time at all, a "little man," no more than three-feet tall, harnessed the horse to the wagon, and off they went. The farmer said very quietly to himself, "Aha, this most certainly is a *lutin*! Now I'll find out where they go." Every now and again, he lifted the covers slightly and saw the horse streaking along as though the Devil himself carried the animal.

The man's house was not far from the sea. Suddenly, the wagon rode onto the water. Amazed, the farmer reached down. Since hay wagons are built low, he was indeed able to feel the chilly water. Then, he heard "Whoa!" and the wagon stopped. The *lutin* put the reins down. The little man jumped off the wagon—Ploop!—onto the water, lit a small lantern, and walked away from the wagon.

The farmer looked out to sea and saw nearly fifty small lights twinkling on the water as the little people gathered in the night.

The farmer had heard that a *lutine*, a female mischief-maker, if captured, could be ransomed for a barrel of gold pieces. But at the moment, he didn't even dare move much less try to outsmart these clever, mischievous creatures. If he moved, he would break the spell and sink immediately. He didn't make a sound, and the horse didn't even move a hair.

After an hour or so, a pale light suddenly approached the wagon, and the little man returned. He boarded the wagon, climbed on the seat, and started back. He drove the wagon back to the farm and into the barn, put the horse in its stall, fed and cared for the animal, and carefully braided its mane before scurrying out of the barn.

That farmer never rode in the back of that wagon again, at least not during the night with a *lutin* at the reins.

He'd had such a fright when he found himself out to sea that he dared not return. The farmer may not have been happy with the answer he found to his question, but there it was.

The *Chasse-Galerie*
La chasse galerie

Some say that in the North there are but two seasons, winter and summer, and that summer comes only for a few days in July. With nothing to do on the farms all winter long and no income to feed their large families, French-Canadian men headed for le chantier. The logging camps of Québec and northern New England became their homes from early November until the April meltdown. That was a long time away from their loved ones, and the temptation to find supernatural means to visit was sometimes just too strong, especially around the holidays.

*J*oe Dupuis was a cook in the logging camp. Every New Year's Eve, all the men gathered around the big cook stove to enjoy the warmth of the night fire and the heat of the Jamaican rum they'd saved for the occasion. One particular year, all the warmth had made Joe a little light-headed. He stretched out on his bearskin blanket, just to rest his eyes a little before he and the men headed off to wish a happy New Year to the men of a neighboring camp, what they call *chanter la guignolée.*

When Joe woke up, he was alone and all his friends had left. He bundled up and made his way outside. No one could be found. Then, he spied Baptiste Durand, who anxiously approached Joe.

"We're on our way to Lavaltrie. You want to come?" he asked impatiently.

"Lavaltrie!" Joe exclaimed. "Why that's a hundred *lieues* from here. It'd take you two months to get there—even if there was a way out. Besides, we've got to work the day after New Year's."

Baptiste had other ideas. "Fool! You go by birch-bark canoe, not by sleigh. With a few good paddles, we'll be there and back by six in the morning."

Now, Joe understood. This was an invitation to run *la chasse-galerie*. These men would be making a pact with ... the Devil himself. Would Joe be willing to put his immortal soul in danger, all to spend a few hours with his girlfriend and family?

"Let's go, you wet hen!" cried Baptiste."In *la chasse gallerie*, we can travel at fifty leagues an hour, so there's no danger of returning after sunrise. The only other conditions are that we avoid church steeples—no problem with strong paddlers like ourselves—and not let the name of God cross our lips. So we watch our language! Look, there's already seven of us, but we've got to have an even number. You'll make it eight. Think of your lovely girlfriend, Liza Guimbette. She'd love to see you tonight..."

Well, the arguments were too much for a brain already weakened by rum, so Joe tumbled behind. He and Baptiste soon reached the clearing. The other six men were waiting impatiently, paddles in hand, around the big birch-bark canoe used for the log drive.

"Everybody in the canoe!" shouted Baptiste, as he took the leader's place in the rear. "Now repeat after me..."

"Satan, ruler of hell," they intoned. "We promise to give you our souls, if between now and our return at sunrise, we say the name of God or touch the cross on a steeple. On this condition, you will transport us to where we want to go and will return us to this camp. Acabris! Acabras! Acabram! Fly us over the mountains!"

With that, they were off, flying five hundred feet above the ground. The night was beautiful, and in the full moon, they could see the forest below almost as well as in daylight. But it was incredibly cold. Frost covered their beards, and the wind cut their breath. Each stroke of the paddles propelled the canoe.

They soon saw the lights of a small town. Telephone poles came into view and ... the church steeple. They stayed clear of it and flew on. Baptiste decided that, just for the fun of it, they would skim over Montréal. At this, Joe almost lost his chewing tobacco. The few people out at that late hour watched in amazement as the loggers flew overhead. They knew what these men were up to.

Then the paddlers settled into their work. Just as though they were on the river, they began to sing a traditional song that kept the beat of the paddling.

Baptiste kept a steady hand; he knew exactly where to go. "Has he done this before?" Joe wondered.

They had seen a lot of forest and many towns when Baptiste yelled, "Watch out, everybody! We're coming down in that clearing! We'll land here and go on foot to the village."

Sure enough, this was a field belonging to Joe's godfather, Jean Gabriel. The snow reached their waists, and they struggled through it to get to the nearest house. Père Robillard informed them that the young people were all off to Batissette Augé's place in Petite-Misère, past Contrecoeur, on the other side of the river, for a New Year's Eve dance—what was called a *rigodon du jour de l'an.*

Back in the canoe, the men chanted, "Acabris! Acabras! Acabram! Fly us over the mountains!" And off they went again.

A couple paddle strokes brought them to the home of Batissette Augé. They could see the light streaming from the frost-covered windows and hear the fiddle and the laughter in the night. They hid the canoe in the bushes and made their way to the house.

Their arrival caused quite a stir. Père Batissette himself came to greet them."Where did you come from? How did you get here?" he asked.

Baptiste brushed aside all the question. "We've come from far away and are very cold. We'll have plenty of answers later," he said. "But right now, how about a drink?"

As for Joe, he spotted Liza Guimbette in a corner with that Boisjoli boy. Joe walked over, offered his hand, and he and Liza went across the floor. For two hours, they never once stopped dancing. The only ones who weren't happy about the woodsmen's arrival were those *habitant* boys who now sat on the sidelines.

While Joe danced with Liza, he noticed that Baptiste was often near the whiskey bottles, and that worried him considerably. When four o'clock chimed, Joe nodded in Baptiste's direction. Then, he went over to tell him it was time to leave. Joe finally had to grab Baptiste's arm and drag him along, all the while trying not to be obvious in front of the guests. Joe never said goodbye to anyone—not even Liza. That's probably why she decided to marry Boisjoli.

The paddlers loaded the stone-drunk Baptiste into the canoe. There was just enough time to make it back, and the moon had disappeared behind the clouds.

"Baptiste, ol' buddy," Joe cautioned," make straight for Mount Royal just as soon as you can spot it!"

"Hey, mind your own business," Baptiste shot back."I know what I'm doing."

"Acabris! Acabras! Acabram! Fly us over the mountains!" And they were off.

The navigator's hand was no longer steady. They flew less than a hundred feet from the church steeple of Contrecoeur. Then, instead of heading due west, toward Montréal, Baptiste steered them up the Richelieu River. On Beloeil Mountain, they missed the temperance cross by only ten feet!

Joe could see Montréal in the distance and yelled out, "Turn right, turn right, Baptiste. Head toward Mount Royal before you send us all to hell!"

Instinctively, Baptiste turned toward the city. But they hadn't climbed high enough to make it over the mountain, and the canoe plunged into Mount Royal. Fortunately, the snow was soft and no one was hurt. When they had dug their way out, Baptiste wanted to go to town for a drink. He began to swear, and before he could utter the name of the Almighty, the men gagged ol'Baptiste, tied him up like a sausage, and dropped him into the bottom of the canoe.

"Acabris! Acabras! Acabram!" the men said soberly.

This time Joe took the helm. They made good time, despite the loss of one man. They knew what was at stake. In fact, they soon forgot about Baptiste, who, strong as he was, struggled with the knots that bound him. They paddled furiously and made good time. They were startled a while later when Baptiste stood straight up in the canoe and let out a blood-curdling yell. He grabbed his paddle and swung it over the men's heads like a madman. Luckily, they were almost back to camp. Joe, while dodging the flying paddle, made a false move, and the canoe went down into a large fir tree. The craft and its passengers tumbled from limb to limb like partridges full of bird shot.

Joe felt as though he was falling into a bottomless well and passed out before he hit the ground. He woke up in his bed at camp. Miraculously, no one had broken back or limb in the fall, but there were aches and pains aplenty and more than one black eye. The important thing was that the paddlers had come back to camp instead of going to hell. Joe didn't even care what stories the guys who found them spread around the camp. They could say what they wanted about Baptiste and himself and the others rough-housing and drinking Jamaican rum out in the snow bank. Let them think what they wanted.

Many years passed before Joe told the story to anyone. And he always ended his tale to the younger loggers with these words, "If you want to go see your girlfriend in the middle of winter, make sure you don't have a drunk for a guide. Better still, wait until spring to embrace the love of your heart and avoid risking your soul."

Brash Irreverence

****

These stories reflect underlying attitudes somewhat subversive to the institutions that held such a firm grip on people's lives. These institutions—the church, courts, and government—provided stability and structure to everyday life, and officially supported the values by which people lived. They were also, however, sometimes seen as the instruments of oppression. On the one hand, the Catholic Church offered a gateway to wonder and mystery, a sense of ritual and awe, and a social context of belonging and community. But on the other hand, this same Church, like its governement counterparts, had an oppressive and paternalistic side, a human foce that imposed countless petty rules and fostered stifling superstition and an enormous sense of guilt.

The French Canadians of yesteryear believed that the courts, the government in general, and, especially, the Church were all God's representatives on Earth, an attitude that did not preclude poking fun at the foibled of "important people" like priests, doctors, lawyers and judges.

This kind of "contradiction" is, indeed, a basic human characteristic. Even today, people complain about doctors and layers in one breath, and fondly hope—in the next breath—that one of their children may one day join the ranks of this elite.

The String of Trout
La brochée de truites

An attempt to reduce the priest, the influential representative of the all-powerful Catholic Church, to a more human scale, this story is one of many suggesting that innate intelligence and resourcefulness can be a match for "omniscient" authority.

Once there was a man in a village in Québec who lived not far from the church. He loved to fish for trout at a nearby brook, and he often sent his little boy to take a string of lovely trout as a gift to the parish priest.

One day he called his son, "Come here, my boy. Take these nice trout to the priest."

To his father's surprise, the little boy replied, "No, Papa, I don't want to go!"

"What did you say? Now stop your foolishness and take these trout to the priest!"

"No, Papa, I don't want to!" he said again.

"And why not, my boy? What is the problem?"

"There's no problem, Papa. I just don't want to go."

"Oh come now. Look at how beautiful they are. Go just this once and I won't ask you to do it again."

The boy grabbed the trout and stomped off toward the priest's house. When he arrived, he knocked, opened the door, and saw the priest seated at the far side of the room.

The boy flung the string of trout onto the floor, slammed the door shut, and started walking away.

The priest rushed to the door, swung it open, and shouted, "Come back here, young man! You come back here right now, and I'll show you there is a proper way to bring a string of trout to your priest!"

The little boy walked sheepishly back into the priest's house. "Very well," the priest said, "I'll show you proper behavior. First, sit down in my chair. Yes, yes, go ahead! Now, you'll pretend that you are the priest, and I'll pretend to be a little boy."

The priest picked up the string of trout, went outside, and knocked on the door. The boy, playing the priest, said, "Come in, little boy!" The priest entered and bowed politely to the boy. "Good day, Reverend Father, my papa has sent you a lovely string of trout!"

The boy accepted the trout, reached into his pocket for a quarter, handed it to the priest, and said, "Thank you, my boy, this is to pay you for your trouble."

The priest was taken aback. "Ah, so now I understand why you behaved as you did. You want to be paid for your trouble, do you? Very well, I'll pay you, but come here." The priest stood in front of a small table, put a quarter on one corner of the table, a half-dollar on another corner, and a dollar bill on still another corner.

"Now, you will choose your payment, young man. If you take the quarter, you will go to heaven when you die. If you take the half-dollar, you will go to purgatory. And, if you take the dollar, you will go to hell, that place of eternal fire and punishment. So my boy, make your choice."

The little boy looked from one piece of money to another, thinking this situation over carefully as the priest waited impatiently. Suddenly the boy scooped up all three—quarter, half-dollar, and dollar—shoved the money into his pocket, looked up at the priest, and said, as he ran out, "Now, I can go wherever I want!"

Justice Is Blind
La justice est aveugle

✦✦✦✦✦✦✦✦✦✦✦✦✦✦✦✦✦

A peasant's daydream or a jab at the judicial system? Or perhaps both. How many peasants—in another time or this—manage to create this type of outcome in a similar circumstance?

There once was a poor devil of a peasant who had nearly drunk away all his worldly goods and was left with only a spring calf. So he set out to sell the calf and make a few coins. As he walked along, he met the village doctor, who he'd known for a long time, and said, "So my friend, wouldn't you like to buy a nice calf this morning?"

"A calf, how much?"

"One *écu*, that's a good bargain?"

"Sold! Here's an *écu!*"

As he paid the peasant, the doctor told him to take the calf to his house since he had to visit sick people and did not want to backtrack.

The peasant kept walking with the calf and presently happened upon the notary, another old acquaintance. "So my friend," he greeted him, "wouldn't you like to buy a nice calf this morning?"

"How much would it cost?"

"Just one *écu*, a real bargain."

"That surely is a bargain. Here's an *écu!*"

Like the doctor, the notary told the peasant to take the calf to his house, since he had an important appointment to draw up a will for a dying person.

As the peasant continued down the road to the outskirts of the village, he met a lawyer he knew. "So my friend, wouldn't you like to buy a lovely spring calf on this fine morning?" he asked.

"A calf, how much?"

"One *écu*. A real bargain"

"A bargain? That's a giveaway! Here's an *écu*. But take the calf to my place. I'm on my way to town for a trial."

When the peasant reached the village, he went to the tavern and drank until the money ran out. As the sun disappeared in the evening sky, he made his way home with the calf.

The doctor, the notary, and the lawyer were stunned when they discovered the calf had not been delivered. They each decided to set an example and have the dishonest vendor arrested. The peasant, upon learning that he would have a bone to pick with the judicial system, decided to entrust his defense to a crafty lawyer from a nearby town. A bad case deserves a good lawyer!

This lawyer, having heard his new client's story, nodded his head and said, "Your case, sir, is not an easy one to defend. You have roundly mocked the professions, and that is serious. In this instance, there is only one thing to do. In court, each time the judge or the lawyer asks you a question, answer only, 'Waank, Waank, Waank.'"

On the day when the case went to court, the attorney for the plaintiffs, addressing the peasant, asked, "Sir, did you, in fact, the other day sell a calf to the plaintiff, the doctor here seated?"

"Waank, Waank, Waank!" the peasant replied meekly.

"And also to the second plaintiff, the notary here seated?" continued the attorney.

"Waank, Waank, Waank!" the peasant replied in that meek tone of voice.

"And what is worse, did you not also sell the same calf to the third plaintiff, the lawyer, my colleague here present?"

"Waank, Waank, Waank!"

"But to none of the plaintiffs did you deliver the calf, as you were, of course, obliged to do?"

"Waank, Waank, Waank!" the defendant replied once again as he kicked the bench. *Bang!*

"What?" the judge said, awaking with a start. "What is the defendant saying?"

"Waank, Waank, Waank!" the peasant said yet again.

"Your Honor," the lawyer explained, "this case is about a calf that the defendant sold to the three plaintiffs."

"My faith, now there's a well-stocked calf!" the judge commented.

"Waank, Waank, Waank!" the peasant continued. And "Waank, Waank, Waank!" over and over and over again until the judge could stand it no longer. In answer to every question, it was always the same stupid, "Waank, Waank, Waank!"

Finally, bewildered and fed up, His Honor forthwith passed judgement, "Gentlemen, you can clearly see that this man is crazy. In the name of the saints, he must go in peace, and we must never discuss him again."

Overjoyed at having won the case, the lawyer for the defense turned to his client: "Well old pal, that was a slick escape. You made fools of those gentlemen of the professions. Now that you are free, you must pay me for my services."

"Waank, Waank, Waank!" the peasant replied, assuming his most foolish expression yet.

"Here now!" the lawyer said with a jaundiced smile, "You can plainly see that the judge is no longer here. Let's discuss our business seriously!"

"Waank, Waank, Waank!"

"That'll be ten francs."

"Waank, Waank, Waank!"

"Come now! Don't you know who I am? I'm the one who won your case for you."

"Waank, Waank, Waank!"

"You animal, will you stop that? If you make me mad, I'll make you pay through the nose if I have to."

"Waank, Waank, Waank!"

And that's the only response the lawyer could get. When he knew it was no use, he finally left. In this trial, as in many others, justice was indeed blind. It could not thwart the lawyer's tricks nor his client's wiles.

The Indian and the Pastor's Cow

L'indien et la vache du curé

▚▚▚▚▚▚▚▚▚▚▚▚▚▚▚▚▚

Like "The String of Trout," this story shows someone flouting disrespect to an established authority. But the different element—the main character is an Indian—suggests that the teller (in this case my papa, Gérard Parent) is rooting for the Indian against the priest. Perhaps, the teller wishes that he had the opportunity, or brashness, to act in a similar fashion toward the priest, or that he, like the reluctantly converted "savage," could stand outside the Catholic Church's considerable sway. (M.P.)

a poor Indian on the brink of starvation stole the pastor's cow. When the pastor found out, he went to the Indian's house and confronted him.

"Is it true that you stole my cow?

Yes, it is," the man replied.

"You can't do that! That's wrong!"

"Really? Why is that?"

"Well, because, ah, at the end of the world, we're all coming back to be judged for our misdeeds and you'll be …"

"Are you sure," the Indian interjected, "that we're all coming back?"

"Yes, of course I'm sure that we all come back to be judged for all the ..."

"Fine. When your cow comes back, then you take it."

Tales with a Moral

✦✦✦✦✦✦✦✦✦✦✦✦✦✦✦

Some stories have morals, or teachings, about human behavior that are quite simple and straightforward. If we find ourselves "pulling for" the old man in "The Poor Man's Bean," for instance, perhaps it's because of a wish or hope that such a good-hearted person, who is trying to do a decent thing—feeding his children— will be rewarded.

In "Little Thumbkin," the obvious lesson is the timeworn, "obey your parents or you'll get into trouble," though we realize at the story's end that Thumbkin will continue to get in trouble for a long time to come. Could it be, then, that the moral here is aimed at parents?

Furthermore, the "moral" of some stories exceeds expected retribution. In "The Secret of the Animals," a character forcefully learns that certain human bonds are betrayed at a cost, which far exceeds "one shall reap what one sows." Although folktales are normally considered simple stories, these tales suggest a "moral" more complex than meets the eye.

The Secret of the Animals
Le secret des animaux

This story was told by Prudent Sioui, a métis of the Huron people of Laurette, Québec. Folklorist Marius Barbeau notes that stories of the métis, passed on by the elders, contain ancient elements of kings, kingdoms, and castles that can be traced back to France and of the Native American tradition, where animals talk and leaves possess healing powers.

Once upon a time there were two orphans. One day the older brother said to the younger, "We are indeed so poor that we will soon die of hunger!"

"What can we do?" the other asked.

"Well, we could earn a living by begging, but you would have to be blind. If you will trust me in this, I will show you how it is done. But first, I must put out your eyes. Then, good people will have pity on us and will give us alms. I guarantee you that we will make money; in fact, we'll make lots of money."

The younger brother, who had always been respectful of his older brother's ideas, answered, "OK, go ahead, but only on one condition: you must never abandon me, or I will die."

So his brother put the young man's eyes out; and off they went from city to city, begging for their sustenance.

At the end of seven years, they had not only survived but had accumulated a handsome sum of money. But the elder brother had by now become quite tired of having to lead his younger brother around. As they walked along a river one day, the older one pushed his brother into the water. The lad was thrown downstream, unable to contend with the current. Soon, the river became shallow; and, as the blind brother thrashed about, his hand struck a branch. He grabbed the tree and pulled himself out onto the shore. He felt night approaching and, not wanting to be prey for the wild animals, located a tree and climbed as high as he could.

At least I will escape this night from the ravishing beasts, he said to himself.

Three animals—a lion, a bear, and a wolf—came along the path and stopped beneath the tree to chat. The lion said, "I have a secret."

The bear chimed in, "I have one too."

And the wolf added, "Well, so do I!"

The lion had been first to speak; so his friends said, "Tell us your secret, and we will tell you ours."

"Well," the lion said, "as you know, the king of the Kingdom of the Three Afflictions is ill. His sickness appears to be incurable. But I know how to heal him."

With little urging, the lion explained, "Under the king's bed there is an enchanted frog. If someone took it away, the king would be instantly cured."

Now, it was the bear's turn. "I know that the frog in the castle is the fairy who drinks the water and dries the land. If her stomach is slit, all the water will pour out, the rains will fall, the springs will gush, the rivers will flow, and the ocean will breathe causing the tides to surge."

The wolf, not wanting to be outdone, hurried to tell his secret. "The oldest prince has been blinded," he said.

"If someone rubbed his eyes with a leaf from this very tree above us, the prince would recover his sight."

The three had no sooner shared their secrets than they departed, each in his own direction, to search the forest for prey. From his perch high above the animals' heads, the blind man had been listening. Now, he lost no time. He plucked a leaf and rubbed his eyes. Lo and behold! His sight was restored.

"Fantastic!" he cried out. "Now if the wolf told the truth, the others must not have lied either." Picking another leaf, he hid it in his jacket.

Early the next morning, he climbed down from the tree and headed for the castle.

"Your prince is blind," he told the guards. "I too was once blind. I know the secret of his condition, and I can restore his sight."

"How can you restore his sight," they jeered, "when the wisest of men from throughout the entire earth have been unable to help him?"

"Take me to him. I will apply the seeing leaf!"

So they took the young man to the prince, and he rubbed the eyes where darkness had settled. Suddenly, the prince cried out with joy. He could see! His vision had been restored to that of a normal fifteen-year-old. So pleased was he that the prince showered his benefactor with *écus* and lavished gifts upon him. Then, the prince asked if the healer could, perchance, achieve similar results with his old father, the king, who had suffered for a long time from an unknown illness.

"I could cure him," the stranger responded confidently. "But you must leave me alone with him for a few moments, and you must permit me to open the shutters."

After some hesitation, the prince agreed to leave his father alone with the healer; but, as to opening the shutters, well that was another matter altogether. For many years now, the king would not permit the light of day to enter the castle because he did not want to witness the great affliction of his kingdom caused by the terrible drought.

As soon as the young man entered the room, he reached under the royal bed and grabbed the frog that hid there. The king immediately felt an enormous relief. Drawing the frog to himself, the young man then concealed it under his shirt. The king thought he was cured. Yet, when it came to giving his consent to opening the shutters, the king was adamant. No window in his castle was to be opened. So the young man threw the frog back under the bed, and the king instantly became ill again.

He was now worse than before. The king, in fact, could barely speak. "Good physician," he muttered, "I bend to your wise wishes. Open the window if you must."

The young man threw open the shutters and let in the light of day. Then, grabbing the frog again, he threw it out. From the king's tower it fell one thousand feet to the church steeple, where it was impaled on the weather vane. At once, the rains poured from heaven, the brooks gushed forth from the earth, the rivers overflowed, and the oceans produced their tides.

Without fanfare, the young man soon set out on his way along the path leading to the forest. There, he met his brother who had been attracted to the city by rumors of wonders produced there.

"Well, hello, Brother!" the elder said. Then, astounded that the younger man had regained his sight, he asked, "Since when are you no longer blind?"

"Since you broke your promise and abandoned me, you miserable brother!"

The cruel one threw himself at his brother's feet. He also noticed his brother's pockets seemed particularly full.

Tearfully, he begged forgiveness as he coveted the jingling *écus*.

"Where do all these riches come from?" he asked, still kneeling.

"They come from the tree of secrets," the young man responded.

As soon as he learned where this tree of secrets was located, the older brother set out through the forest to climb it himself.

When twilight came, the lion, the bear, and the wolf returned along their usual path. They were in a grumbling mood. Someone, some nosy busybody, must have discovered their secrets. They were in a very bad temper. Stopping at the foot of the tree where they first made their revelations, they noticed the man who waited there.

"Vengeance!" they cried. "It is he who betrayed us. He took the leaf and murdered our friend the frog. Devour him!"

And so they did.

Little Thumbkin
Petit Poucet

✤✤✤✤✤✤✤✤✤✤✤✤✤✤✤✤

Petit Poucet, the French equivalent of Tom Thumb, is in fact closer in translation to Little Thumbkin, the name used here. This story, however, leaves many unanswered questions. For example, how does Thumbkin carry a man-sized basket and climb a fence the height of a bull? And why do the parents become involved in a job and forget the son they set out to find? This is not your usual "do what your parents tell you" sort of tale.

Once there lived a man and a woman. Their only child, a little boy, was very small indeed, so small—about the size of a thumb—that his parents named him Little Thumbkin.

At noon one day when the father went to work in the fields, the mother said, "Little Thumbkin, go take dinner to your father. He's out there, at the other end of the field; but be careful not to go through the paddock where we keep the red bull. He is very mean and will go after you."

And so Little Thumbkin set out with the meal. But like so many children who obey only when it pleases them, he cut right through the paddock, just to see if the bull would come after him. The red bull, of course, was watching. No sooner had Little Thumbkin jumped the fence that the big red bull, having already spotted Little Thumbkin, began to bellow and run. As he ran, the boy realized that what his mother had said was true after all. Thoroughly frightened and unable to go further, he hid under a cabbage leaf, thinking he would be safe.

The bull passed Little Thumbkin. But realizing he had been tricked, he came back on his tracks and bellowed, "Boo-oo-oo! Where is Little Thumbkin so that I might eat him? Boo-oo-oy!" He sniffed and scratched and got very close to the boy's hiding place.

Watching the bull paw the ground, Little Thumbkin rolled himself even smaller under his leaf. The bull, madder than ever, leaned over to smell the cabbage, licked the leaves, and ate the whole plant ... with Little Thumbkin in it! The bull swallowed Little Thumbkin!

That put Little Thumbkin in quite a predicament. What to do in the belly of the bull? There was neither door nor window, and the heat was suffocating. Then, he remembered that his mother, that morning, had tied his sweater with a pin. Grabbing the pin, he jabbed the lining of the bull's stomach. A great shake threw Thumbkin upside-down. The bull, stung by the pin, set off running, jumping, and bellowing in anger. Each time he slowed down, Little Thumbkin gave him another jab with the pin and off they went again!

The father, surprised not to have gotten his dinner, returned home before the usual time. Hungry and unhappy, he asked his wife to explain this negligence.

"Negligence!" she exclaimed. "Why Little Thumbkin set out at noon with your dinner in his little basket!"

Now, the father too was worried. "What! He isn't back yet? Something terrible must have happened to him."

The frightened parents set off to find their son. They scoured the fields and woods but could not find a trace of their child. They returned late in the day and saw the bull in his paddock, raving like he had lost his wits.

"What's gotten into the bull that he should be running so?" the father asked.

"He ran and bellowed all afternoon," replied the mother. "You have to wonder if he hasn't come down with a strange ailment."

"Well, running wild the way he is, he can't live much longer," said the man. "He's already dead tired. We'd better finish him off right now."

The man went into the house and got an ax and a long knife. He then quickly butchered the animal. Having severed the carcass, he loaded one half onto his shoulders, and his wife took the other half. They headed down to the river to wash the fresh meat before salting it.

Little Thumbkin, still reeling, had not said a word, but as soon as he opened his eyes, he realized that he was inside the section of the bull his mother was carrying. He began to sing out loud:

"Bear on, bear on, old bearer!
You don't know whom you're bearing."

His mother, hearing someone sing, turned around. Seeing no one, she became concerned and called out, "Who's that? Who's talking?"

No answer. She started off again, but the voice came back:

"Bear on, bear on, old bearer!
You're moving right along."

Stopping again and putting down her load, the old woman muttered, "You just wait, you teaser, until I get hold of you!"

Little Thumbkin was careful not to say anymore. His mother, thinking she had been hearing things, started back down the path. Immediately she heard:

"Bear on, bear on, old bearer!
I can't wait for you to put me down."

"Are my ears buzzing, or I am losing my mind?" the woman asked no one in particular as she stepped up her pace to join her husband at the river. Arriving out of breath, she dropped her side of beef into the water; and it would have sunk had she not held on tight with a strong hand.

Bending down, she was surprised to see something bobbing about in the water. She looked more closely and cried out, "It's our child, and he's going to drown!" Little Thumbkin had floated out of the side of beef and was taking a forced bath, yelling with all his might. His mother grabbed him, and seeing that he needed a good scrubbing, undressed Little Thumbkin right there in the river and washed him with a firm hand, all the more that she was not in a good humor.

"That will teach you to disobey your parents!" she said.

The Poor Man's Bean
La binne du pauvre

A poor man, having exhausted all resources, seeks supernatural help. He is given "tools" but that does not signal the end of his troubles. He must encounter and prevail over human obstacles, including his own wife, to finally change his situation. He is guileless, good-hearted to a fault, and truly believes in God. His faith is held up as an example of the simple, straight-forward belief that can carry even the most downtrodden man through life's difficulties.

Once upon a time, there was a man who had as many children as there were rocks on his land. He was at his wit's end wondering how to feed them all. So he decided to plant some beans, and one of his bean plants sprouted and kept climbing and climbing. It climbed right into the heavens. So he said to his wife, "I'm going to go up and ask for God's help."

"You old fool. What kind of idea is that? Ask God's help! It takes an old fool to come up with something like that!"

"Well, I'm going."

So he started climbing up his beanstalk, and he climbed and climbed. He finally reached heaven and knocked at Saint Peter's door.

"Yes, what do you want?" Saint Peter asked.

"Well, I'm the man who has as many children as there are rocks on my land. I can no longer feed them all. So I've come to ask for God's help."

"Ah, then I'll go tell God about this. You'll get some help."

Saint Peter went off to speak to God. "What shall we give this poor man, Lord?"

"I know, give him this table. And tell him that all he has to say is, 'Table, table, fill yourself!' and the table will be filled."

Saint Peter carried out God's orders, but the man couldn't go back down the beanstalk carrying his table. So he was forced to take the long way—the back road that wound back down to Earth. When he was halfway home, the man said, "I'll have to try this table out. Table, table, fill yourself!" At these words, the table filled with a feast.

"Now there, I can live well with this."

So he went on his way. At dusk, he arrived at a hotel and asked for lodging. Then he added, "I'm not alone."

"How is that?" the innkeeper asked.

"I have a table."

"Just put it right there."

"Listen," the man added, "don't say 'Table, table, fill yourself!' Just don't say that."

"Ah no, of course not!" the innkeeper replied.

A chambermaid listened to all this.

Around nine o'clock, the man said, "I'm very tired. If you could show me to my bed, I'd like to go to sleep." He went to his room, found a nice bed with clean white covers, and was soon asleep and snoring.

Then the chambermaid said to the innkeeper, "This would be a good time to try out that table of his."

"Sure. Why not!" he replied. "Table, table, fill yourself!"

And, of course, food instantly covered the table. The chambermaid said, "This table would come in very handy for us. Let's keep it."

"Yes, but it doesn't belong to us," he replied.

"We've got one just like it. Let's take this one and replace it with ours."

And so they did. The next morning, the man left the hotel with their table—not his own—on his back. When he arrived home, his wife was standing at the window and saw him coming. She hollered to her children, "Look at the old fool arriving with a table. He thinks we'll be able to live with a table. Ah, old fool of old fools."

When he came in, she said, "You old fool, what do you think you're going to do with that table?"

"You'll soon see, just wait. Come here," he said. "Watch this."

"Table, table, fill yourself!" And, of course, nothing happened. He tried again. "Table, table, fill yourself!" Nothing. "Table, table, fill yourself!" Still nothing. "Ah! A dirty trick they've played on me. They've stolen my table. I'm going to ask for God's help again."

So he climbed all the way back to heaven on his beanstalk. When he arrived, he knocked on Saint Peter's door. "Good day, Sir," Saint Peter said. "What is it you want today?"

"I'm the man who has as many children as there are rocks on my land. I want to ask for God's help."

"But didn't we give you a table?"

"Someone stole the table."

"I'll go talk to God about this then."

Saint Peter went and talked to God. "What shall we give him this time?"

"Let's give him this donkey," God said, "All he'll need to say is 'Donkey, donkey, empty yourself!' and the animal will give him silver coins."

"That's good," Saint Peter said and led the donkey out to the old man.

"This time, all you have to say is 'Donkey, donkey, empty yourself!'"

The fellow went on his way, again having to take the long road back because of the donkey. At about the same spot as the previous day, he said to himself, I'll have to give this donkey a try. "Donkey, donkey, empty yourself!" At these words, out of the donkey's backside fell a big pile of silver coins. "Well, I can certainly live well with that!"

Soon, he came to the hotel and again asked for lodging. "I am not alone, though," he pointed out once again.

"What do you have with you?" the innkeeper asked.

"I have a donkey."

"Well then, we'll just put it in the stable."

As they walked over to do so, the chambermaid followed to listen. And the old man said, "It would be best if you did not say, 'Donkey, donkey, empty yourself.'"

"Oh, of course not," the innkeeper replied.

They went back in. Again around nine o'clock, the old man grew sleepy. They showed him to a room. Exhausted, the old man soon feel fast asleep.

Then, the chambermaid said, "Let's give that donkey a try."

"Alright by me," the innkeeper replied.

They made their way back to the stable and the girl said, "Donkey, donkey, empty yourself!" And, of course, the donkey produced another pile of silver coins. "We've got a donkey that looks exactly like this one. Let's switch them and keep this one."

"Well, you know, it's not really ours," the innkeeper said.

"But don't you think," she retorted, "that the boss would like this one much better?"

"OK, suit yourself," he said.

She switched the two donkeys. And the next morning, the old man set out with what he thought was his own donkey. His wife again saw him coming.

"Here comes the old fool now, this time with a donkey. And what are we supposed to do with a donkey? Old fool of old fools."

When he arrived, she greeted him as warmly as usual, "So you old fool, what do you plan to do with that donkey?"

"Just wait a bit, I'm about to show you." He led the donkey into the room and said, "Donkey, donkey, empty yourself!" And the donkey emptied himself in the only way he knew how. So the old man tried again, "Donkey, donkey, empty yourself!" but again got the same results. "They stole my donkey! I'll go and ask for God's help again."

Once again he climbed his beanstalk until he arrived at Saint Peter's door. "And what do you want now?" the saint asked.

"I'm the man who has as many children as there are rocks on my land."

"But we've already given you a table and a donkey."

"Well, all that was stolen from me."

So Saint Peter went and reported this to God. "So Lord, what shall we give him this time?"

"Let's give him this stick. All he has to say is 'Strike, stick, strike!'"

Saint Peter brought the stick out to the old man and told him what to say. The old man could have climbed back down the beanstalk with the stick in one hand, but he decided to take the same long road back as he'd taken the two previous times. When he arrived at the place where he'd tested the table and the donkey, he decided to test his stick. "Strike, stick, strike!" And the stick began to strike everything in sight. So he stopped it and kept walking. At nightfall, he came to the same hotel. "Can I sleep here tonight?" he asked.

"Certainly," the innkeeper replied.

"But I'm not alone."

"What else have you got?"

"I have a stick."

"Just put it in that corner over there."

"OK. But I really wish you wouldn't say 'Strike, stick, strike!'"

"Well, of course not!"

The chambermaid heard all this. Around nine o'clock, the old man said, "If you'd show me to a bed, I'd surely like to go to sleep."

So they showed him to a room with a good bed with clean white covers. Soon, he was snoring, and the chambermaid said to the innkeeper, "This would be a good time to try out that stick. Strike, stick, strike!" And lo and behold, the stick began to strike her repeatedly. "Please go tell him to come stop this stick. Hurry!" she said. The innkeeper sprinted up the steps to wake the old man. "Your stick is beating my girl. Come stop it!"

"I will if you give me back my table and my donkey." Then he said, "Strike, stick, strike again." Now the stick began to strike the innkeeper until he pleaded, "OK, we'll give you back your table and donkey. Please just stop that stick."

The old man stopped the stick.

The next morning he took his table, his donkey, and his stick and headed home. His wife, who again saw him coming from a distance, said, "Look at the old fool coming along with a table, a donkey, and a stick. What does he think he's going to do with all that?"

When her husband arrived, she began berating him. He said, "You just wait. Today you'll see something quite different. Watch what happens this time. Table, table, fill yourself!" And, lo and behold, the table did indeed fill itself with food. The old lady's jaw dropped.

"What about that donkey?" she asked.

"All right, hang on!" he said, "I'm going to show you. Let's set this up so that we don't drop any of the silver coins. Donkey, donkey, empty yourself!" And, of course, the donkey let loose a load of silver coins.

"So my sweet old wife, I'm an old fool, is that right?"

"But you haven't showed me what that stick does," she said.

He grabbed the stick and commanded, "Strike, stick, strike!" At these words, the stick moved menacingly toward the old lady. The good-natured old man, willing to let bygones be bygones and happy to finally have fortune smiling upon him, quickly stopped the stick. He had made his point. And his wife only occasionally called him an old fool after that.

Scoundrels, Heroes, and Semi-Heroes

✢✢✢✢✢✢✢✢✢✢✢✢✢✢✢✢✢✢

Occasionally, the line between heroes and scoundrels blurs. In this chapter, some obvious and very definite scoundrels—the beggar in "The Friend of Thieves" and the prince in "The Two Magicians"—and a distinct hero, Ti-Jean, in "Ivory Mountain," appear. Other not-so-obvious heroes are also found in these tales—the dwarves in "The Talking Mirror," and Mama in "Ti-Jean, Mama, and the Collector."

Imagine that a hero is on one end of theoretical spectrum and a scoundrel on the other end. The characters in this section often slide from one endpoint to the other.

These stories also present legal, moral, and emotional dilemmas. But instead of providing ultimate answers to thorny questions, they move readers to ponder life's ambiguities and complexities.

The Bear and the Fox
L'ours et le renard

With its talking animals and hidden truths, this story is of interest because it resembles Aesop and Jean de Lafontaine's stories on the one hand and American Indian tales on the other. Some readers might dismiss the story's logic. Why, they ask, should the fox antagonize the bear by awakening him? Why doesn't the fox just steal the butter and leave well enough alone? Or does the story strike upon deeper psychological truths and strange ways of human behavior?

There once was a bear and a little fox. One winter's morning, the fox stopped before the bear's den and, sitting on a snow bank, began to howl. The little fox howled and howled until finally the bear, sticking his head out, said, "My little friend, what is wrong that you should howl so?"

"Ah, I have so many problems!" the fox answered.

"Which problems?"

"I've been asked to be a godfather, but I'm not sure I want to go.

"Hey, buddy, go ahead! You'll get a lot to eat and fill your belly. If someone asked me, I'd be happy to go instead of licking my paw all winter."

"Now that sounds like good advice," the fox said as he left.

But making a half turn, he came back on his steps and quietly entered the bear's pantry. Finding a tub of butter, the little fox ate his fill. When he was finished, he came back out on the snow bank and began to howl again. Sticking his head out of the den, the bear asked, "What did you name your godchild?"

"I called him Just-Begun."

"That's a very nice name, my little fox. If he's just begun, he has a long way to go."

"Bear, you are so right."

The next morning, the fox returned to the same snow bank in front of the bear's den, sat down, and began to howl. The bear woke up. He stuck his head out of the den and said, "My little friend, what is wrong that you should howl so?"

"Don't even talk to me about it! I've got so many problems. They're asking me to come be a godfather again, and I don't want to."

"Ah, go ahead! They take really good care of you when you're the godfather. You come back with a well-rounded belly."

The fox left right away and, making a half turn, went straight to the bear's pantry, where he ate butter. By the time he finished, only half a tub was left. Sitting on the snow bank, he started to howl again. From the cave, the bear stuck his head out and asked, "What did you name your godson this time?"

"I called him Half-Way."

"Half-Way! That's a fine name, my little fox. With a name like that, he still has a long way to go."

"Bear, he doesn't have as far to go as the other one named Just-Begun!"

The next day, the fox was back to his howling, going at it stronger than ever on that same snow bank. Howl and howl, he did. The bear woke up; and, sticking his snout out of the den, he asked, "My little friend, why do you howl so much?"

"There is no end to my being called to be a godfather, but I don't want to go."

"You shouldn't have to be begged so. When you're the godfather, you always come back drunk. If they asked me to go, I wouldn't stay here licking my foot. No, I wouldn't have to be pulled by the ear very long."

The fox made a half-turn. Returning to the bear's pantry, he ate the rest of the butter, right to the bottom of the tub. When he had finished, he returned to the snow bank in front of the bear's den and began to howl one last time. The bear stuck his muzzle out and asked, "What did you name your godson?"

"I called him Bottom-Licked."

"Ah, what a lovely name, my little fox!" the bear answered. "It's always on the bottom that we get the best licks. I wish someone would ask me to be a godfather! I'd like the change, I who spend the winter licking my paw."

When spring came, the bear went to his pantry to get his tub of butter. He was sorely disappointed to find it empty, clean-licked to the bottom. So the bear went to find the fox and said, "My little friend, I can see you played a trick on me this winter when you were called to be a godfather. Your godsons were named Just-Begun, Half-Way, and Bottom-Licked. Well, it's my turn to be a godfather. I'm going to start right away."

"Ah! my good bear, don't eat me up when you are so angry. Tired as you are from your trip, you should lie down here, next to me; and when you wake up, tomorrow morning, we'll figure out who ate your butter."

The bear thought for a moment and then agreed. Very tired indeed, he lay down and fell fast asleep. While the bear slept, the fox buttered his behind with fresh, spring butter that he had stolen elsewhere during the night.

When the bear awoke, he smelled butter all over his backside. Very humiliated, he said, "How stupid I am! I must have eaten my butter myself during the winter, while I was half asleep."

The fox departed and soon had a head start. Before disappearing, he turned around and said to the bear, "You are not very smart, believe me! Now lick your paw!"

Since that time, the little fox is much smarter than the bear. And during the winter, the bear still licks his paw.

The Friend of Thieves
L'ami des voleurs

✦✦✦✦✦✦✦✦✦✦✦✦✦✦✦✦✦

Though the cheated bumpkin in this story derives no benefit from the following moral, it may, in fact, give mild comfort to the reader and to this tale's many listeners through the centuries. And the lesson is: Even though scoundrels do sometimes prevail, their villainy is occasionally directed toward someone who seems deserving of it.

Once there were two neighbors, one a wealthy merchant, the other a beggar. The people in the village often said that the merchant was unscrupulous in his business dealings. And the beggar was rumored to be light-fingered. He always roamed at night and returned with a full sack on his back at dawn. Since his arrival in the village, some strange robberies had been committed.

A country fellow came to the merchant's place one day to buy a sheep. The merchant took him to the pen and sold him a nice sheep. They tied the animal's feet, and the fellow carried it out on his back.

No sooner had his customer left than the merchant ran to the beggar's place. "I just sold the best sheep in my pen to a bumpkin. You could relieve him of his heavy burden, if you catch my drift; and you and I could share the profit."

"Got it!" the beggar said and instantly reached into his sack, pulling out a brand new pair of shoes. Instead of following the country fellow along the path, he darted through the fields to reach the nearby forest. At the edge of the woods, he placed one of the shoes in the middle of the path. About a half mile later, he dropped the other. Then, he hid in the brush.

Upon entering the forest, the bumpkin noticed the shoe, stopped, and, as he moved on, said to himself, A shoe, a nice shoe. Too bad there isn't a pair!

When he walked deeper into the forest and saw the other shoe, he put the sheep down and retraced his steps to fetch the first shoe he'd seen. He returned for his sheep that had now fallen into the beggar's hands. The animal was, of course, nowhere to be found.

The bumpkin, quite determined to own a sheep, returned to the merchant the very next day. "Sir," he said, "I had some very bad luck yesterday. My sheep got lost in the woods. Do you have another nice one like it that you could sell me?"

"Certainly, my friend. I have one just like it. You could almost mistake one for the other. Come have a look!"

The fellow—oblivious to the fraud—bought the same sheep he'd bought the day before, paid cash, and set out again with the animal hoisted over his shoulders. The merchant again ran to his accomplice and repeated his previous offer.

"It's a deal!" the scoundrel said. This time, he loaded some chunks of salt pork into a basket and hurried to the forest to scatter them along the path. Placing his basket in the middle of the path, he again hid in the brush.

The bumpkin came along, noticed the chunks of salt pork, but didn't pay much attention to them. Until, of course, he saw the basket. He once again put the sheep down, grabbed the basket, and again retraced his steps.

"Nothing like these for making soup!" he said, gathering the chunks.

When he returned to the middle of the forest, the sheep was gone. He was stunned. And this, the second one he'd lost!

The next day, he showed up and purchased—a third time—a sheep *very much* like the first two he'd bought. As soon as the man left with the sheep on his back, the merchant alerted his partner, the beggar, and again offered him an equal share. Ever ready, the rogue dashed through the fields. This time, though, he took nothing.

In the middle of the forest, he hid in the brush near the path. When he saw the bumpkin approaching, he started bleating like a sheep. "Baa-aa-aa. Baa-aa-aa."

The other fellow stopped to listen. "Aha, there we are," he said, "now I can recover my other sheep." He put down the sheep he'd been carrying, plunged into the brush, and searched in every direction. The beggar pounced on the fellow's sheep, seized it, and scurried off.

When the bumpkin returned to the path, empty-handed, his sheep had disappeared. Dumbfounded, he completely gave up trying to purchase a sheep, since he had no luck with it. And he was not seen in the village again.

The merchant, instead of sharing half the profits, as he had agreed, gave only one-third to the beggar, who walked away without objecting. But the next day, three sheep were missing from the merchant's pen, which seemed to him rather fishy.

Driven by suspicion, the merchant went to look under his pillow for his wool sock, where he stashed his money. The sock was empty! He dashed to his neighbor's to find the beggar gone, the house empty, and a placard the beggar had nailed to the door.

The placard read:
> *Thieves, be they poor or rich,*
> *Have the Devil as a friend;*
> *But he who robs last,*
> *Also laughs last, in the end.*

Ivory Mountain
La montagne d'ivoire

The turning point in this story seems at first almost an aside. The somewhat abbreviated conclusion to the adventure strongly suggests which of Ti-Jean's actions the teller thinks is truly the most "heroic."

There was once a very old and very wealthy king. His daughter, a sweet and beautiful girl if ever there was one, had been captured by a dragon. She was being held on Ivory Mountain, and the king had tried everything to rescue her, but to no avail. Finally, in despair, he proclaimed that he would give his daughter's hand in marriage, as well as half his fortune, to whoever could rescue her.

Now, in this kingdom there lived a poor woodcutter, his wife, and three sons—fine, brave young fellows named Pierre, Paul, and Jean. Pierre offered to rescue the princess under one condition— the king must pay him the promised sum immediately. The king agreed, showering Pierre with gold coins. However, Pierre, unwise and carefree, spent all the money.

Paul came forward next and said, "Since we live on an island, I'll need a boat to venture forth. So I need the money to build one."

The king, desperate and a bit gullible, gave him bags full of money without even counting it. When the boat was finished, Paul pulled up the anchor, lifted the sail, and set out to sea. After a few weeks, the ship wrecked, and the best that Paul and his crew could do was save themselves.

Jean, the last of the three sons, approached the king. "I won't waste your money. I will take only as much as I need," he said. "My arms, my legs, and my brain will do just fine. Though it won't be much to brag about, I think I can do better than my brothers."

So he set out, made his way to his godmother's house, and asked, "Could you tell me where Ivory Mountain is?"

"No, I cannot," she replied, "but my sister, the Insect Fairy, may know something about that. Why don't you pay her a visit?"

Jean hit the road again and walked and walked for a long time until he finally reached a cottage with a thatched roof. He knocked at the door and was invited in by an old woman.

"Your sister, my own godmother, told me that you might know where Ivory Mountain is," Jean said.

"No, I don't know," she replied, "but if you're willing to walk for a long, long, long time, you'll find a little green house perched near a frightful abyss. Listen closely and you'll hear the voices of the fish. My cousin, the Fairy of the Fishes, lives in that house."

Jean took to the road once again and walked for miles and miles and miles before he finally arrived at the Fairy of the Fishes' house.

"And good day to you, dear Fairy Lady," he said most graciously. "Your cousin, the Fairy of the Insects, sent me to see you. She said you'd know where Ivory Mountain is."

"Oh, my gentle young man, I know nothing about it. But my grandmother, the Fairy of the Birds, is well informed about such things. She can tell you the long and the short of it. But I must warn you that you'll have to walk almost a thousand leagues to get to her place. I'd suggest you put on the Seven-League Boots that you'll find behind the door. Take them and good luck!"

With renewed courage, Jean put on the Seven-League Boots and started walking yet again, and walking and walking until it seemed the walking would never end. He reached a village and stopped to eat and rest in a stable yard. He looked across the yard and could not believe his eyes. There, on top of a dung hill, lay a man's corpse. "Why in God's name don't you bury this corpse?" he asked the villagers.

"That's the corpse of a man who didn't pay his debts," one man answered. "It's the custom here to leave debtors and robbers out to be devoured by birds of prey."

"Bury that man!" Jean said. "I'll pay for the burial and pay his debts."

Jean used the king's money to give the man a proper burial, and then he left to continue his journey. After walking for days and nights, he arrived, at long last, at the house of the Fairy of the Birds.

"Good Fairy Lady," Jean said, "your grand-daughter, the Fairy of the Fishes, told me you'd know where Ivory Mountain would be. Could you tell me how to get there?"

The old fairy started whistling, for this is how she called her subjects to her. The birds gathered on the field and she asked, "Do any of you know where Ivory Mountain is?" There was no response, but the eagle had not yet arrived. She whistled again, and the eagle appeared.

"Do you know where Ivory Mountain is?" she asked.

"Yes, I do."

"Would you show this young man the way?"

"I'd be glad to."

"Jean, climb up on the eagle's back," the fairy said. "He'll show you the way. Here are some chunks of beef to keep beside you on the trip. Whenever the eagle cries 'W*aack*, W*aack*!' cut off a piece of beef and feed it to him. Do you understand?"

"Yes," Jean said, and off like a storm, the eagle and his brave rider went. Through long days and nights, man and bird journeyed in full flight, crossing vast distances. But the mountain was nowhere in sight and the eagle had almost finished the meat. "W*aack*, W*aack*!" he cried again and again. When the meat was gone, Jean grew deeply troubled. How could he possibly feed his eagle?

The bird flew down, down, down and finally perched in a tree. It turned out that the tree had long been enchanted. Each time a bird alighted on it, a great flood occurred. Now water cascaded from everywhere, a deluge that soon reached up to Jean's neck. He was quite sure his next breath would be his last.

Then, something amazing happened. Out of the torrential waters a small white boat appeared. As Jean awaited his last moment, the ashen sails floated toward the tree. A sailor dressed in white stood on the boat's keel and spoke to Jean. "Do you recognize me, my friend?"

"No! Who are you?"

"I am the one you took pity on. You paid my debts and had me buried. Thanks to you, my body now rests beneath the earth; but my spirit still lives, and I can help you. I'd like to repay you. Hop in, and I'll take you to the seaside, to the foot of Ivory Mountain where the dragon is holding the princess prisoner."

Jean quickly boarded the white boat and stood next to his grateful friend, the spirit. Carried by the winds and buffeted by the waves, they bobbed about for a long time. Suddenly the sea calmed, and they sailed right to the foot of the Ivory Mountain. The spirit in white spoke once again.

"The dragon is aging," he said. "He has little strength to do battle. You should have no trouble running him through with this spear I've brought you. As soon as you step onto the beach, you'll find three small golden eggs. Pick them up, break the shells, and you'll find three iron clamps. Attach them to your boots, and they'll help you climb to the top of the mountain where the castle sits.

"When you get to the door, you'll see the wizard who guards the entrance. Here, in this pouch, is an ounce of gold dust. Throw it in his face; he'll fall backwards, blinded, and you can go by. At the very top of the crystal tower, you'll see the lovely captive with another wizard by her side. She cries constantly, the poor girl, because her captor is a hard, cruel being. Touch her with this magic stick, and the wizard will turn to stone."

With these words, Jean set foot on the beach and turned, but not in time to say goodbye to the spirit, who had disappeared leaving behind the shiny white boat. Jean found the golden eggs on the beach, broke their shells, and followed the spirit's instructions.

It was truly amazing how everything fell into place. With the iron clamps from the golden eggs, Jean swiftly climbed the mountain. Encountering the first wizard, Jean blinded him with the gold dust. Next, he reached the princess' chamber, quickly touched her with the magic stick, and turned the second wizard to stone. The dragon appeared; and, as the spirit had said, the creature was no longer the fearsome adversary he once was. Jean ran the dragon through with his spear and rescued the tearful princess. She instantly fell in love with him, simply out of gratitude. She was so beautiful and sweet and in need of protection that Jean thought of nothing but marriage to the princess.

And that's what happened. The wedding was lovely; and, when the old king passed away, Jean succeeded him to the throne in the Kingdom of Dreams. And he and his bride lived a long and happy life.

Drip-Nose and Golden-Fish
Morvette et Poisson-d'or

✦✦✦✦✦✦✦✦✦✦✦✦✦✦✦✦

A fairly pathetic figure at first, here's a hero whose life changes dramatically because of a fairly simple gesture. But then he has to grow into the role.

Once upon a time, there lived a poor fisherman and his wife. Their only child, a young man, was called Drip-Nose, because ever since he was very young, his nose constantly dripped, and he was always wiping it with his hands. It was truly a pitiful sight.

One day, while the fisherman was in his boat preparing to go fishing, Drip-Nose, who was watching him, said, "Today, Father, take me fishing with you. I'm old enough to help you make our living."

"Oh, be quiet, Drip-Nose. All you ever do is sniffle, drip, and wipe your nose. You'll scare the fish away!" his father replied.

The young man started crying and went back to the house. His mother, who had pity on the boy, went to speak to her husband. "Come now, just take him out once and see how it goes. He's old enough to learn how to fish. If you never show him how to do anything, how do you expect him to take care of us in our old age?"

His wife's reasoning persuaded the fisherman to take his son aboard. But by the time they reached the fishing area, he was overcome with revulsion. He quickly returned to shore and outfitted a small boat for Drip-Nose so the boy could fish alone.

"Manage as well as you can!" the father said as he untied the line and pulled his son's boat toward the current. "But to be safe, don't go out beyond The Points at land's end."

Overjoyed, the boy stopped wiping his nose and started rowing toward The Points. Then, he stopped rowing, let the boat drift, and threw in a line with a baited hook. He was soon startled to get a big bite. He quickly yanked the line up and was quite surprised to see a small golden fish emerge from the water.

He was doubly surprised when the fish spoke to him. "Drip-Nose, my good fellow, throw me back into the water where I came from!"

"Are you kidding?" the boy replied. "You're my first fish, I'm going to keep you. Tough luck, you let yourself get caught!"

"But I'm so small, barely a mouthful. It's hardly worth it."

"But you're so fine-looking. You're not like me, pitied by everyone," the boy answered.

"Come on, be a good-hearted boy!" the golden fish said. "Do what I ask and you won't regret it. Anything you wish for when you say, 'Golden-Fish!' you shall have, for I am the magic spirit of the waters."

Drip-Nose hesitated. He wiped his nose. Then, taking pity on the little fish, he threw it overboard and started fishing again. But he got no other bites and was sorely disappointed. What would his father say? Suddenly he cried out, "Little Golden Fish, if you keep your word, fill my boat with fish!"

No sooner had he said the words than his boat over-flowed with fish. He was barely able to row. Drip-Nose's father, responding to his son's call, pulled his own almost-empty boat up to his son's. He was stunned to see how well Drip-Nose had done. He took part of the marvelous catch, and the two of them, satisfied with the day's work, returned to shore.

The fisherman said, "My fine boy Drip-Nose, we've got fish to spare. It's been a long time since something like this happened. Hey, why don't you take two of the biggest fish and give them to the king on my behalf!"

Drip-Nose had nothing better to do and followed his father's suggestion. He arrived at the castle, dropped his load, and knocked on the gate. The king's daughter came to the door.

"Good Princess," Drip-Nose said, "my father sent me to bring you these fish."

"Where did you get these beautiful fish? I've never seen anything like them."

"In the water," Drip-Nose replied.

"Now isn't that quite an answer!" the princess retorted as she burst out laughing.

He had no idea what to say. Embarrassed, he started wiping his nose again.

"What is your name?" she asked with disgust.

"My name is Drip-Nose, at your service."

"Ha, ha!" she mocked. "Now there's a lovely name!" And she turned around and slammed the door in his face.

Disappointed and angry, Drip-Nose called out, "So that's it, you ridicule me. Well, I can have anything I wish for. You'll discover that at your own expense! Through the power of my little Golden Fish, you'll be punished. Before long you'll have something to remember me by."

Some months later, distress filled the king's castle. The princess had given birth to a child, a beautiful baby boy.

Lacking any convenient explanation, the king consulted an old fairy hag. Even for her, the birth was a mystery. To find the child's father, she suggested, the king should give a crystal ball to the child and then have all the young men of the kingdom file past. The child, the old fairy promised, would surely hand the crystal ball to his father.

The king issued a proclamation requiring all the young men of the kingdom to come to the castle on the day after the next full moon. Failure to obey this order would result in death.

On the ordained day, as the fisherman was obediently preparing to accompany his son to the castle with the other young men, he felt embarrassed. Before they entered, he said, "Son, with your dripping nose, it's best that you not go any further than the entrance. Hide behind the door because, if he lays eyes on you, the king will surely throw you out."

Drip-Nose followed his father's instructions to the letter. He slipped into the crowd and then hid behind the door, crouching to stay out of the king's sight. Then, to everyone's surprise, the princess's baby boy straightened in his mother's arms, slid to the floor, and, escorted by the princess, started walking. He carried the crystal ball directly behind the door to … Drip-Nose.

The king saw Drip-Nose—now ashamed, embarrassed, and wiping his nose more than ever—and flew into a violent rage. He ordered his guards to seize the impostor, put him in a boat, and abandon him to his own devices far out to sea. The worst thing for the king, though, was that nothing could hold back the princess and the child with the crystal ball. Drawn by an irresistible power, they followed the condemned Drip-Nose and boarded the boat with him to share his fate.

The child was soon seized with hunger. He cried, demanding food. The princess curtly reminded Drip-

Nose, "At the castle door, you bragged that you could have anything you wished for. So why can't you get some fresh gruel for your son?"

Drip-Nose thought of Golden-Fish. He asked for some gruel for the crying child and plenty of tasty food for the hungry princess. After a delicious meal, the princess said, "Since you can have anything you want, why don't you wish for a castle and wish that the castle be more beautiful than my father's, and that it be located right in front of his?"

Drip-Nose called upon Golden-Fish and asked that his castle be one hundred times more sumptuous than the king's and be transported, along with himself, the princess, and the child, to the very front of the royal castle.

The next morning, the king awoke to a blinding light shining from the castle in front of his own. In the sunrise, the new castle glittered brightly with diamonds and precious stones. The king sent his servants to ask who lived in this magic place. To his great surprise, he learned that it was none other than Drip-Nose, the princess, and the child with the crystal ball.

The princess, always on the lookout for new marvels, spoke to Drip-Nose once again. "Since you can wish for and obtain anything you want, why don't you wish to have your nose stop dripping?" So accustomed to sniffling, dripping, and wiping, Drip-Nose hadn't even thought of this though it was surely the first thing he should have wished for.

So he immediately asked Golden Fish to cure him of his affliction and transform him into a prince worthy of the princess and their child. And the young fisherman with the dripping nose became a handsome young man, elegantly dressed and with the finest manners.

The king, much enchanted, quickly made amends with his daughter's spouse. But it was now important to find Drip-Nose a new name befitting his status as heir apparent to the kingdom. And what name did the young man choose? None other than Golden-Fish, his "first fish," whose life he had wisely spared and whom he would always hold in fond memory.

The Two Magicians
Les deux magiciens

This is a traditional tale of an anti-hero, a protagonist who lacks the virtues and estimable traits of a traditional hero. The prince is a brilliant scoundrel; the king, a greedy fool; the magician, a wise master who allows a personal vendetta to cloud his judgment. We want a Foolish John to win out over the capricious forces of the unjust abuse of power and wealth, but this bully.... Well, sympathy for him develops nevertheless, because the prince is cunning and, besides, he knows a good princess when he finds one.

There once was a king who had but one child, a son. One day, he said to the boy, "Handsome Prince, I would like to educate you according to your tastes. What would you like to learn?"

"Well, my father," the prince answered, "I would like to know about good and evil. And since no one knows more about these subjects than the old magician who lives in the mountains, I choose him as my teacher."

Early the next morning, the prince departed. Arriving at the magician's home, he knocked on the door. "Hello, Teacher," he said.

"Hello, handsome Prince! What do you want with me, hermit of the mountains that I am?"

"I seek instruction in good and evil," the young man declared.

"*Pristi*, you are ambitious!" the magician answered. "Both good and evil, eh? The good won't be difficult; it is accessible to everyone. But evil ... Ah! that is another matter. It is not easy. You must truly have an innate ability in order to enter its mysteries."

Well, the young prince must have had such talent because, in very little time, he learned the secrets of the magician's wondrous arts. When, at the end of his studies, he believed he knew as much as his master, he said goodbye and returned to the castle. Greeting his father, he said, "My father, I have learned all I care to know about good and evil."

"*Tonnerre!* You really seem to have benefited from your studies! Now could you tell me, in particular, what you learned?"

"You will see tomorrow when I change myself into a white horse. Take me into town and sell me for one hundred and one *pistoles*. But make sure you remove the saddle and bridle and keep them for yourself."

The next day, the king—in disguise, of course—went into town with one valet, who led the white horse that had appeared in his stable. The king put the horse up for sale, the most beautiful white horse anyone had ever seen.

No sooner sold, unsaddled, and unbridled, the horse reared, broke loose, charged off, and disappeared. The buyer immediately started chasing the horse but shortly came upon a handsome prince.

"Sir Prince, did you happen to see a white horse go by, for he has escaped me?"

"Yes, in fact, I did! The six winds carried him along."

"Well, if that's the case, then I will never catch him!"

"My opinion precisely. My dear friend, you had best forget about your horse. He has the Devil in him."

The next morning, the prince said to his father, "To-day, I will change myself into a black horse. Go once more into town and sell me for one hundred and one *pistoles*. But once again, keep the bridle and saddle for yourself."

"Understood!" the king replied, delighted with his son's prowess.

In the meantime, the old magician had heard about the actions of his disciple. He said to himself, I have yet to give him his best lesson. Taking his saddle and bridle, he went into town early. Soon he came upon the king, his valet, and the black horse.

"Is your black horse for sale?" the magician asked.

"Most certainly! He is black as a jay; his legs are slender; and his head, proud. His equal is not to be found. But I will sell him to you for a mere one hundred and one *pistoles*. Take it or leave it."

"Here are the *pistoles*," the magician said. "This horse is now mine."

"But," the king said, "I keep for myself the saddle and the bridle."

"As you wish. I have better ones to break in badly trained horses."

With a steady hand, the magician replaced the king's saddle and bridle with his own, and off he went with the black horse. As he led him to his stable in the mountains, the magician muttered, "You will see, my scatterbrained friend, what awaits you! You will suffer as I see fit."

To his valets he commanded, "I forbid you to give drink or food to this horse during my absence, which will last several days."

While the magician was away, the valets noticed as they passed through the stable that the horse was rubbing himself against the wall. The poor beast was hungry and thirsty. They said, "The master has been absent longer than usual, and his horse is dying of hunger and thirst. Ah!

If he only knew! We have to do something. Let's take the horse out of the stable and give him a drink."

They took him to the stream, but the horse didn't even lower his head to look at the water. One valet said, "Some horses, thoroughbreds especially, refuse to drink when they have saddle and bridle. Let's remove them so that he may quench his thirst!"

No sooner were the saddle and bridle unbuckled that the horse reared, let out a string of farts capable of knocking over a wall, and jumped into the river, swimming off like a fish.

The magician, returning that night, asked, "And about my horse, you haven't given him anything to drink, I hope?"

The sheepish valets answered, "Bad news! He was rubbing so hard that the walls shook. Worried that we were, we took him to the stream, but he wouldn't drink. The only thing to do was to unbridle him. But once unbridled, he dove under the water like a fish."

Furious, the magician hired one hundred fishermen with nets and told them to catch all the carps in the river from the first to the last. The prince, who had, in fact, transformed himself into a carp, was drawn up with the others to the water's edge. He now became a yellow diamond amid the pebbles on the beach.

A prince's emissaries, seeking precious stones for the princess he was about marry, noticed the beautiful yellow diamond. They picked it up and took it to the princess. Overjoyed, the princess hid the diamond in her bodice. To her great surprise, she felt the diamond move. Taking it again in her hand, she watched it change into a little man, who, once on the floor, grew before her eyes into a charming prince.

"Do not fear, princess! I changed myself into a yellow diamond on the river's edge to escape the fisherman's net.

The old magician, who is on my trail, is about to arrive here. To undermine his ruse, permit me to change myself into a seed in the heart of this apple. Seeing it, the magician will recognize me. You must then take the apple and smash it against the wall. The seeds will fly about, and I will be the smallest. I will fall at your feet. Put your foot on me!"

The next morning, the magician arrived at the princess's castle. "Princess," he asked, "you wouldn't happen to have received a beautiful yellow diamond that I lost yesterday on the river's edge? I cherish that diamond like my own eyes!"

"Yes," the princess said, "but I myself have lost it."

"Well, well!" the magician exclaimed, "he's changed himself into this red apple!"

Quick as lightning, the princess threw the apple against the wall. It exploded into pieces, and the seeds scattered. The smallest seed fell near the princess, and she covered it with her foot.

Changing himself into a rooster, the magician pecked left and right at the seeds. But the littlest seed transformed into a fox. The fox pounced on the rooster. He devoured the bird, putting an end to the magician.

A man once more, the prince stood before the princess, thanking her profusely. When he could think of no other way to say thank you, he decided there was but one remaining possibility—asking her hand in marriage. She did not miss her cue. Soon, a royal wedding occurred with great rejoicing.

After all, princes are made for princesses.

The Baker Gets Rich
Le boulanger s'enrichit

✤✤✤✤✤✤✤✤✤✤✤✤✤✤✤

In this classic tale of good and evil, the trusting and courageous baker is amply rewarded while the dishonest and cowardly thieves receive their just desserts. Truly a children's story, the real fun here comes from the parade and chatter of the animals— the perfect setting for a skit.

There once was a baker who learned that the people of the neighboring village named Poverty had fallen on hard times. Poverty was very small. The men were not much for hard work, and the women were not industrious. Worst of all, thieves infested the surrounding forests.

"If I went there to sell a cart full of bread," said the baker to himself, "I couldn't help but make new customers for myself." He baked up a good batch of bread and loaded it in his cart. Still early in the morning, he set out for Poverty. The road was long and bad, and the baker arrived at his destination late in the afternoon. But in no time at all, he had sold all his bread—although everyone bought on credit.

"Hey, you don't get anywhere in business," he told himself, "when you refuse to give credit."

With the bread gone, it was time to leave. After his horse ate some grass along the road, the baker hopped into the wagon, snapped his whip, and headed for home.

He hadn't gone ten paces when a bull blocked the road. "Good baker," the bull said, "misery has reigned here for a long time. I can't hold out any longer. Thieves have stolen everything. I am the only horned animal left. I am certain the people will kill me and make me into stew. Have pity on me! Take me far from this village."

"What will the townspeople say if I get involved in their affairs?" the baker asked.

"Don't worry. They will think that I have fallen into the hands of the forest thieves."

"Get into my wagon," the baker replied.

A little later he met a big dog who said, "Good baker, you are taking the last bull of the village. I protest! For longer than I can remember, I haven't even had a bone to gnaw on. Please let me follow your wagon."

"Do so if you wish," the baker said.

A rooster jumped onto the only picket left standing at the last house in the village. "Good baker," the rooster said, "yesterday the thieves took the last chicken from my hen house. I don't understand what is going on. Take me with you!"

"Get up here in the wagon," the baker said.

An *arpent* later, a big rat emerged from the stream. "Good baker," the rat said, "there is nothing left in the village to steal. If you don't take me, I will die of hunger."

"Come up into the wagon," the baker replied once more.

With the rat on board, the cat ran up. "Good baker," she said, "you are taking away the only rat in Poverty. What will become of me? I was letting him get fat before turning him into dinner. Take me with you!"

"Come up into the wagon," the baker answered.

By now the wagon was pretty heavy, and the roads were still bad. Night was fast approaching. What to do? the baker thought. He spotted a small light off the road near the great woods. Reining in his horse, he peered through the night, wondering who or what was out there. Filled with curiosity, he set out across the field, as quietly as he could, to see for himself. Arriving at a small house, he cautiously peeked through the only window. He spied three thieves seated around a table counting their money.

As quietly as he had arrived, the baker stole back across the field to the wagon and summoned all the animals from the largest to the smallest. He told them to be very quiet and follow him. Retracing his steps with the animals in tow, he shared his plan with the beasts and then silently positioned them around the house. The thieves, so engrossed in counting their money, only had ears for the clinking of gold coins.

When the baker signalled, the horse whinnied and beat down the door with his hooves. The bull bellowed and rammed the tiny house. The dog barked and scratched the earth. The rooster crowed and beat his wings. The cat wailed. The rat hissed, "Pss, pss, pss!" as best he could. And the baker ran around the house beating the walls with his stick, crying out, "Thieves! Thieves!"

Panic-stricken, the robbers flew out of the house without even grabbing the money. The baker had no scruples in helping himself to the loot since, he thought to himself, robbing a thief would not be robbery. Now I am well paid, he said to himself, for my cart full of bread.

It was too late to return to the road. But what will I do if the thieves return? Better ready than surprised, he said to himself. Once more, the baker assigned positions to the animals. The dog scurried under the front porch. "Good dog, if they return, bark and bite without mercy," he instructed.

Placing the bull behind the door, he gave this admonition: "Lie here, good bull. If they enter, welcome them with your horns."

Tying the horse to the foot of the bed, the baker said, "You with your sound hooves, give them a good kick!" He assigned posts to all the animals—the cat in the stairs, the rat in the empty fireplace, and the rooster on the chimney top.

No longer worried, he fell soundly asleep.

The frightened thieves hadn't gone very far when they realized their blunder—the biggest of all possible blunders—they had forgotten the loot!

"It's your fault," one robber said. "You're stupid!"

"Stupid! You call me stupid? Why, you're … chicken!"

And so the fight began. *Bang! Bang! Bang!* They fought so hard and so long that both finally fell to the ground unconscious. The third robber decided to make the best of the whole situation and go back for the gold for himself. It was now pitch dark, and only with much groping did he make it back to the darkened house. There was no sound from within. On tiptoe, he moved up onto the porch. Still nothing. Emboldened by the thought of gold, he quietly opened the door and headed for the table.

Suddenly, the bull bolted from behind the door. His kick butted the thief across the room and half way up the stairs. The noise woke the cat who screeched and flung herself into the man's messy hair, digging her claws into his face. Stunned, the thief rolled down the stairs landing headfirst into the fireplace where the surprised rat cried out, "Pss-pss!" biting him square on the nose.

In one immense leap, the robber jumped over the table to the bed where the baker waited, stick in hand. "Thief! Thief!" the baker cried. Getting into the act, the horse administered one swift kick that shot the intruder out the door like an arrow. Fear and cold air cleared the thief's mind, and he was on his feet and about to take off when the dog finally woke up. First, he dug his teeth into the man's coattail, then into the seat of his pants.

"Good God! Mercy!" the thief shouted, thinking spirits had attacked him. The man shot off, but the dog held on. The bull bellowed and followed in pursuit. "Me too!" the horse said. Just to speed things up, the cat, wailing all the while, jumped on the dog's back. "Pss-pss! Not so fast!" the rat hissed as he ran. "Wait for me!"

"*Cocorico! Cocorico!*" the triumphant rooster crowed.

But the baker didn't bother to get up. With his head resting on a sack of gold, he fell back to sleep.

The next morning, the baker hitched up the horse and set out with the animals.

"Pss-pss!" the rat hissed.

"*Cocorico! Cocorico!*" the rooster sang.

When they reached the baker's village, the dog barked; the cat mewed; the bull bellowed; and the horse whinnied. Upon learning how the baker has succeeded in doing good business, the villagers began celebrating his return.

When the townsfolk of Poverty heard what had transpired, a delegation was sent to protest. "Just think of it! The baker took away our dog, our bull, our rooster, our cat—and even our last rat!"

But everything turned out for the best. The baker kept his menagerie and promised to send Poverty a full load of bread. And what is more, he kept his promise.

The Talking Mirror
Le miroir qui parle

In this story another type of hero appears: well-intentioned dwarves who are flawed rescuers. In fact, they seem to have completely failed the damsel-in-distress in their care. But they finally and ironically rise to the occasion simply by admitting their "failure." Part of the enjoyment of this story comes from recognizing variations on the familiar themes of "Snow White," "Sleeping Beauty," and even "Alice in Wonderland."

*I*t had been eight days since a man and his wife had come to live on one of the farms not far from the village. No one knew them, but the news soon spread that their daughter was a remarkable beauty. No one had ever seen such a marvelously beautiful girl as she.

A few days after the family's arrival, the young girl said to her mother, "Mama, today I went to a clearing in the forest and saw some huge raspberries. If you'd like, I could go pick some."

At first, her mother refused, afraid to let her daughter go into the forest alone. But, because of the girl's insistence, she finally relented and allowed her to go, but warned her not to venture too far into the dense woods.

The young girl joyfully took to the forest path and was soon picking raspberries by the handful. She was so busy picking the berries near a tree stump—her bucket nearly full—that she didn't notice a huge, dark, and very deep hole in the ground only inches away. She took another step and was swallowed up, disappearing into the hole.

Dizzy from the fall but not badly hurt, the girl began feeling around for a way out. When she adjusted to the darkness, she saw a wall. Then, a door. She jiggled the handle, and the door opened. And how surprised she was to find a lovely little dwelling, there under the earth! Then she heard a sound from within the house, and three tiny dwarves appeared. Though they seemed gentle, she stepped back cautiously.

One dwarf carried a bundle of kindling branches on his shoulders, and another had a large partridge on his back. They stopped, looked at her, and asked who had shown her the entrance to their secret dwelling. She explained that she'd accidentally fallen into the hole while picking berries and had just discovered it.

She asked them to please help her return home to her parents who would be worried about her long absence. But, the third dwarf replied, "We'll do nothing of the sort right now. I bring important news, and I believe it concerns you. The witch, who is known as Jealous Beauty, is trying to track down a beautiful girl. I'm sure you're the one she's looking for. I saw her leaving your father's house. She could be here tomorrow, though she hasn't come around here since the mysterious death of our mother."

"We suspected her of the crime and chased her out quite brutally. We hope she's lost all desire to set foot in this place again. Stay here awhile. You can take care of the house and prepare our meals. You'll be comfortable and safe here.

"If the witch is desperate or determined enough to find her way here while we're gone, do not open the door.

It will be your doom. We know her dark, evil spells and only want to protect you."

Jealous Beauty lived in a run-down shack on the outskirts of the village. She had a nasty reputation and was rumored as the source of many evil spells. It was whispered that she had been a ravishing beauty in her youth but that a sweetheart she dearly loved abandoned her to marry another. She must have exacted her vengeance because, one year after the wedding, her former lover and his bride came to a most sinister end. People claimed that she'd never ceased taking revenge against beautiful young girls, who all met sudden, unexpected deaths.

Jealous Beauty had been sick in bed for six days. She only arose to sip broth and take various herbal medicines to regain her health. On the sixth morning, feeling somewhat better, she got out of bed and fetched a small locked box at the bottom of an old trunk. The box held some rings and bracelets, a necklace, and a small mirror, which she quickly grabbed to look at herself. No doubt the illness had somewhat damaged her beauty.

After admiring herself, she intoned a somber and bizarre refrain. Speaking to the mirror with a twisted expression on her face, she said, "Little silver mirror, is there anyone more beautiful than I?"

And the mirror answered, "Yes, very near here, a young girl a hundred times more beautiful than you."

On hearing this reply, the witch screwed her face up in a frightful laugh. Uttering harsh threats, she wrapped herself in an enormous black coat, stepped outside, and strutted across the village. When she arrived at the young girl's house, the witch discovered that her rival had gone to pick raspberries. So the witch could not see her that day.

The next morning, Jealous Beauty spoke to her mirror again. "Little mirror, is there, right at this moment, anywhere near here, anyone more beautiful than I am?"

"In the forest nearby," the mirror replied, "there is a young girl a hundred times more beautiful than you."

The witch quivered with rage, wrapped herself in the huge black coat, and stalked out again, this time toward the dwarves' hole. She dropped into the hole, approached the dwarves' house, and knocked on the door.

"Who's there?" the young girl asked, not forgetting the dwarves' instructions not to open the door to a living soul.

"My pretty one," the witch said, "I am a friend and would love to pay you a visit."

"That's impossible. I cannot open the door for you," the girl said.

"Well, if you really cannot open the door, just pass your hand through the small opening in the window. I'll put this precious ring on your finger. Then you'll surely know that I'm your friend."

The young girl, thrilled about receiving a valuable ring, extended her hand to the witch, who placed the deadly ring on her finger. The girl immediately fell lifeless to the floor. Pleased with her latest foul deed, the witch quickly left.

Soon thereafter, the dwarves arrived to discover the young maiden on the floor. As they approached her, one of them noticed the ring. He quickly snatched it from her finger and threw it into the fire. The girl instantly came back to life.

She rubbed her eyes and said, "I'm sorry. I must have fallen asleep." Not wishing to frighten her, the dwarves did not say a word.

The next morning, the witch took her mirror as usual and said, "Little silver mirror, is there anyone near here more beautiful than I?"

And the mirror replied, "In the nearby forest, there is a young girl a hundred times more beautiful than you."

The witch stomped around in a rage. "What, she's not dead!"

She again put on her coat, darted out, went down the dwarves' hole, knocked on the door, and demanded entry. But the young girl refused.

So the witch said, "My poor, dear child, I am your friend, and I've come to bring you a souvenir. Let me pass it to you through the small opening in the window. It's a necklace of precious pearls."

Unable to resist the temptation, the girl let the witch put the necklace around her neck through the opening in the window. The young girl was again thrown lifeless to the floor. The witch fled, and the dwarves soon returned. They realized that the witch had been up to her evil tricks again; and, seeing the necklace, they ripped it from the young girl's neck and threw it in the fire.

The girl instantly awakened and rubbed her eyes. "I must have fallen asleep again."

Again the dwarves said nothing, but they were deeply disturbed by the witch's evil deeds. She was indeed determined to destroy the young girl because of her beauty.

The next day, the witch again picked up her mirror. "Little silver mirror, is there now, anywhere near here, anyone more beautiful than I?"

And the mirror once again replied, "In the nearby forest, there is a young girl. Truth be known, she is a hundred times more beautiful than you."

This time, the witch did not fly into a rage at the mirror's response. "It's the dwarves who thwart my desires," she said. "This time, I'll try something else."

She took a fine, shiny apple and injected a powerful poison into it, took a smaller apple for herself, threw on her coat, and once again made her way to the dwarves' hole. "Open the door! Let me in!" she commanded.

And the voice from inside said "No, I won't open it for anyone."

"What? You won't even open it for me, your friend? Here then, my little one, I'm leaving you this lovely apple. Eat it and you'll see how delicious it is. I must go now."

As the witch turned to leave, she began to eat the other apple. The young girl saw this; her mouth watered. Why not eat the even better apple she'd been given? She reached for the fruit, took a bite, died instantly and collapsed, her body already stiff.

The witch had barely disappeared into the forest when the dwarves returned. This time, they had left early in the morning in hopes of coming back in time to catch the witch red-handed. Too late! All they saw was the young girl stretched out lifeless on the floor with the apple she'd bit into by her side.

One of the dwarves picked up the apple and flung it into the fire. But nothing happened. The apple contained no evil spells; it had simply been filled with poison. The dwarves were discouraged and despondent.

"What shall we do?" the first asked.

"We might have done better to send her back home right away," the second said.

But the oldest said, "We knew she was facing death and we did our best. Whether she was at home or here, the witch would have found a way to kill her. For too long, as you well know, we've put up with having that maker of misery as a neighbor. Let's build a coffin and carry this child's body to her home. There we'll do our best to explain everything and suffer the consequences. Too bad for us if we're punished."

Sadly, they built a coffin and laid the body inside. With great effort, they lifted their heavy load out of the cavern. Then, discouraged and with heads bent low, they carried their burden toward the parents' house. They were moving slowly along the road when they saw a wagon coming their way.

When the driver reached the strange procession, he stopped the wagon. The dwarves asked if the man could please transport them and the coffin to the parents of the departed girl. The driver readily agreed, and they were soon on their way. But rocks and ruts covered the road, and the bumping and jolting of the heavy wagon fiercely shook the coffin and its dwarf bearers.

To their great surprise, upon arriving at the girl's house, they heard a stirring in the box. The violent shaking of the wagon had dislodged the poisoned apple. Yes, the beautiful girl was alive!

The girl's father and mother were more than a bit stunned to see their daughter climb out of the casket. They all joyfully entered the house where the dwarves tried to explain the recent events. They told the young girl's parents that they had kept their daughter in hopes of shielding her from the witch's evil tricks.

The father, so happy to have recovered the daughter he feared was lost forever, sent for the magistrate of the village. He wanted to consult the official about the best way to protect his daughter from the witch's evil spells. It was finally decided that the girl would walk past the witch's house the very next morning and that she would accept the witch's advances. She would be closely followed by law officers who would rescue her.

The next morning, the witch again consulted her mirror. "Little silver mirror, tell me, is there at this very moment, anywhere near here, one more beautiful than I am?"

And the mirror replied, "Look very near, there is a young girl a hundred times more beautiful than you."

Jumping with rage, the witch looked out the window and saw the young girl, who she had believed was finally dead, approaching. "Ah ha, you won't escape me this time!" she laughed menacingly.

The witch took something from her strongbox, wrapped herself in her huge, black coat, marched outside, and bounded to the middle of the path to face the girl. "Well, where might you be going now, my pretty one?" she asked.

"Oh, I'm not feeling well this morning. I thought a short walk would do me good," the girl replied.

"Well, come with me," the witch said with a smile most sweet and cloying.

"No, I think it's best for me to go back home now," the girl said.

The witch cast a furtive glance around her to be sure she could safely cast her spell, saw no one, and said, "My dearest, my lovely, I do so much desire to put this pretty bracelet on your plump, pink wrist."

The girl allowed the witch to do so. Thump! She fell lifeless to the ground.

Two officers dashed from their hiding place behind a hedge, swooped down on the witch, and arrested her. One of them took the girl into the nearest house and tried to bring her back to life. He bent over her and rubbed her hands. Then, one of the dwarves removed the magic bracelet, and the young girl immediately regained consciousness, opened her eyes and smiled.

As for the miserable evildoer, she was taken before the magistrate who condemned her forever to exile in the deepest part of the forest. If she ever returned, she would be locked in an iron cage in the village square. Her old shack was burned to the ground. Her bracelets, necklaces, and the strongbox expired into a column of flames the color of blood that reached the sky.

Two years later, the beautiful heroine married a lord from the region, and the two settled down quite happily.

The couple visited the dwarves often and had a portal of sculpted stone built at the entrance of the underground dwelling in gratitude for all that their small friends had done for the young woman.

The beautiful lady and the lord passed their days in gentle harmony until death forced them to submit to the lot of all mortals on this good earth.

Ti-Jean, Mama, and the Collector

Ti-Jean, Maman et Monsieur l'Intendant

✶✦✶✦✶✦✶✦✶✦✶✦✶✦✶✦✶✦

In this story, the "villain" is referred to as the landlord. But as the title suggests, he may be more accurately described as the "agent" or "collector" for the lord of the manor in the seigneurie *system. Mama, the heroine, acts maternally—if not necessarily legally or morally. Whether or not early listeners of this tale believed Mama had done the right thing probably depended on their feelings about their own landlord, landlords in general, and/or their attitudes toward a system where the majority of people labored under the cruel heel of a collector similiar to the one for whom Ti-Jean provides final comfort.*

Once there lived a boy named Ti-Jean, who was not very clever, and his mama, who, lucky for him, was.

Ti-Jean's dear papa had died years before, and it was Mama who took care of the household.

One day, Mama had to go to town on urgent business. She expected to return in time to settle the monthly accounts with the landlord but gave Ti-Jean instructions in case she was detained. "Tell Monsieur Landlord I'll be back soon, and do make sure he is comfortable," she said to her son as she left.

Ti-Jean quickly said three "Hail Marys" to speed Mama's journey, for he dreaded the thought of having to spend any time with the landlord, who never spoke a kind word to him. The people in the area always said that Monsieur Landlord never entertained a kind thought, let alone uttered a kind word. Ti-Jean and Mama had even given the name "Monsieur Landlord" to their old goat because of the animal's wispy beard and nasty disposition.

As it happened, soon after the church bells had tolled at midday, Ti-Jean was startled by a loud knock. He scurried toward the door in the vain hope that it was anyone but Monsieur Landlord. But, alas, that important person stood, looking down his nose at Ti-Jean and stroking his goatee as though he were the king himself. Ti-Jean, quaking with fear, invited the landlord in, showed him to the best chair, and poured him a cup of tea. Then, he stood off to the side, ready to jump into service if Monsieur Landlord had the slightest need. He offered the great man cheese and bread, then sausage, then cake, and then more tea. All of which the landlord gruffly refused.

As the minutes passed, the landlord shifted in his chair and drummed his fingers on the table. Ti-Jean repeated the offers of food and drink, but the landlord waved him off with growing impatience. Ti-Jean began a string of silent "Hail Marys" as he stood frozen by the awesome responsibility of keeping the landlord happy.

Then, to his dismay, he noticed a fly buzzing around Monsieur Landlord's head. Ti-Jean remembered what Mama had said about ensuring the landlord's comfort, so he inched closer, hoping to draw the fly to himself and away from his guest. But, the fly seemed intent on the landlord's head. Ti-Jean took a wet cloth, wiped the table with it, walked behind the landlord, took a swipe at the fly with the cloth, and missed—scattering crumbs on his guest.

The landlord whirled around in his chair and fixed Ti-Jean with a look that made the poor boy sweat and tremble. Next, Ti-Jean tried to subtly eliminate the pest with a fly swatter, but to no avail. Then, to his horror, the fly landed on the landlord's head. Surely, Ti-Jean thought, Monsieur Landlord's impatience would turn to boiling rage. Determined to follow Mama's instructions and desperate to vanquish the fly, Ti-Jean grabbed a hatchet, swung it toward the target, and neatly chopped the fly in half. He also, ever so unfortunately, chopped the landlord's head in half.

Ti-Jean fell to his knees in terror and confusion and prayed to Mother Mary and all the saints in heaven that they might bring Mama home. When she arrived, carrying sacks full of goods she'd bought in town, Ti-Jean thanked Mary and the saints and blurted out to his mama every detail of the catastrophe.

"My poor Ti-Jean," Mama said, "you are indeed a good, well-intentioned boy; but the authorities will say that your story is that of a madman. Then, they'll hang you for what you've done, though nothing will be gained by adding your death to his. So now, calm yourself, do exactly as I tell you, and thank God above that he has given you a Mama who loves you *and* who has an idea or two in her head."

Next, Mama gave Ti-Jean his instructions. "Now, my dear Ti-Jean, listen closely, do not ask any questions, and do exactly as I say. Do you understand?"

Ti-Jean nodded, his eyes wide open.

"I have some work that I must do here inside the house. You will start by digging two holes, one behind the barn and the other near the pig pen. Dig both holes as deep as your waist, as wide as your shoulders and as long as your Papa was tall. When you're finished, come back in, and I will give you more to do."

Ti-Jean was as strong and willing a worker as he was dim-witted; so Mama knew the holes would soon be ready. She set to work without wasting a moment. First, she prepared Monsieur Landlord for his own final "settling of accounts" and cleaned the house thoroughly.

Then, she dashed outside, out of Ti-Jean's sight, put the ladder up against the far side of the house and fetched an empty water bucket. She brought the bucket into the house and filled it with fresh fish she'd bought at the market that very day. She added water and set the bucket outside near the ladder. Ti-Jean burst through the door. "Mama, I've finished digging both the holes. What must I do now?"

Mama handed him the hatchet. "Now, my dear Ti-Jean, you must put our poor old goat out of his misery. His time has come. One quick blow to the top of his head and he will not suffer. Then you must bury him in the hole you dug near the pig pen. That will be a good resting place for *our* Monsieur Landlord. Be quick about it, and come back in when you've finished."

Ti-Jean went out the door without a question. Mama then dragged the dead landlord's body out the side door, again out of Ti-Jean's sight, and quickly buried him in the hole behind the barn. She smoothed the dirt and spread the surplus around the yard. Then she went inside the house ahead of Ti-Jean.

He came in seconds later to tell her he'd completed his task. "Well done, Ti-Jean," she said. "Now you must stay inside the house while I attend to some chores. When I come back, you must tell me everything that happens while I'm gone. Do you understand?"

"Yes, Mama, I will tell you everything," Ti-Jean replied dutifully.

"Good, my son, you can even sit in your Papa's old rocking chair here by the fireplace and look out the window. Would you like that?"

"Ah, yes, very much, Mama!"

With that, Mama went out the side door, picked up the bucketful of fish, and quickly and quietly climbed the ladder to the top of the house. She nimbly moved to a spot just above the window that Ti-Jean was gazing out of and poured out the contents of the bucket so that the water and fish fell past the window.

Ti-Jean was amazed at this incredible sight and was about to start screaming with delight when he heard a strange voice calling to him from the chimney. Mama had smeared her face with soot from the top of the chimney, pulled the pin from her ever-neat hair and let it hang wildly around her face. She continued to call to Ti-Jean in a shrill, eerie voice that would have raised goosebumps on Monsieur Landlord himself. As Ti-Jean looked up the chimney in terror and awe, he saw a creature like he'd only imagined in nightmares, and began screaming. Mama quickly wiped the soot off her face, tied her hair, and clambered down the ladder to ask Ti-Jean why it was he was screaming so.

He told her the whole story. She assured him that he had nothing to fear from that witch since she herself knew the creature quite well. They went out, gathered the fish, cleaned them, and Mama made a delicious supper for them. She said she'd never heard of fish coming out of the sky, but that these certainly tasted as good as any she'd eaten.

Three days later, when the high magistrate came to their door, Mama told Ti-Jean to answer the man's questions as well as he could. She opened the door, led the official to a chair, poured him some tea, and asked if she could be of any help.

"Perhaps you can, Madame. It seems Monsieur Land-lord is missing. Foul play is strongly suspected. So we are seeking any information that you might have. May I ask you a few questions, Madame?"

"Ah, yes, absolutely. I would like to be of help if I can."

"Very well, then. When did you last see Monsieur Landlord alive, Madame?"

"Oh, it's been a good while, at least three or four weeks."

"I see. Excuse me, Madame, no disrespect intended, but I must ask if you yourself had any particular rancor in your heart against Monsieur Landlord."

"Oh, Monsieur Magistrate, I must tell you truthfully that I did not especially like him. My son can even tell you that I often referred to him as 'the old goat.' But I certainly did not wish him dead, as God is my judge."

"Well, of course, and thank you. It is no secret that he was not a well-liked man. And there is of course a long road between dislike and murder. Do you mind if I ask your son a few questions, Madame?"

"No, sir. He is a good, honest boy and will answer your questions about the old goat—I mean about Monsieur Landlord as well as he can."

"Very well. Now, my boy, have you recently seen Monsieur Landlord alive?"

"Yes sir, just a few days ago. But then I split his head with the hatchet and haven't seen him since."

The magistrate looked in shock at Mama, who quickly moved to Ti-Jean.

"Oh, my God, my dear sweet boy. On what day did this happen?"

"Oh, Mama, it was the same day that I told you it had rained fish when you were out doing some chores."

Mama turned to the confused magistrate, shrugged her shoulders, and continued to question Ti-Jean.

"Son, what else happened on that day?"

"Well, Mama, that was the same day that the witch was in our chimney."

At this point, the magistrate took Mama aside.

"Excuse me, Madame, but is your son completely all right, if you know what I mean?"

"Well, the fact is, sir, that he is not very clever. Not at all clever, in fact. But he always tells the truth as well as he's able, if you know what I mean."

"Yes, certainly, Madame. Allow me to continue the questioning, if you don't mind."

Mama nodded. Monsieur Magistrate approached Ti-Jean. "Young man, would you mind telling me why you split Monsieur Landlord's head with an axe?"

"Oh, you see, it's because he had a fly on his head and Mama had said that I should make sure that he was ..."

"Now I understand!" Mama interrupted. "Honorable Magistrate, please come outside. I think my son can show you something that will answer your questions and clear up some confusion."

She led the magistrate into the yard toward the pig pen. Ti-Jean, a bit confused himself, followed and awaited Mama's next instructions.

"My dear boy, please take the shovel and dig up the old goat whose head you split because his time had come."

The magistrate watched closely as Ti-Jean dug up the white, furry body of "Monsieur Landlord," the goat.

Mama turned to the magistrate. "You see, we've always called our goat by that name because of the similar beard and personality. Now then, would you like to ask my boy any other questions? I'm sure he'd give you some very interesting answers."

"I'm sure he would, Madame. But I think I shall pursue my inquiries elsewhere. Sorry to have taken so much of your time."

So it was that from that day on that Mama always gave Ti-Jean very clear, detailed instructions. And she always made it a point to be at home during the next landlord's monthly visits.

Love Prevails

Love is an ingredient that unsurprisingly flavors many tales, especially the Ti-Jean stories. And what is there to say about love? Regarding this great mystery, perhaps it's only possible to speculate or suggest. These stories seem to imply, among other things, that the great blessing we call love comes to those who are pure of heart and know the pain of its absence, (as in the story "Words into Flowers"), to those dreamers willing to believe in the impossible (as in "The White Cat"), to those lovers who persist in their devotion to their beloved in the face of scorn (as in "The King Makes a Proclamation").

Words into Flowers
Les paroles de fleurs

✤ ✤ ✤ ✤ ✤ ✤ ✤ ✤ ✤ ✤ ✤ ✤ ✤ ✤ ✤ ✤ ✤

It is interesting to note that, in this Cinderella variant, the young girl is already a princess, and yet is still oppressed by a wicked stepmother. Is this an avowal that royalty does not necessarily shield one from suffering? Was this a novel idea at the time it was first told? Does the princess prevail simply because of her basic goodness?

Once, a widowed king had a lovely daughter, his only child. He decided to remarry, and his new wife was also widowed and had a daughter about the same age as the king's own child.

While the king was hunting—his favorite pastime—the new wife treated his daughter like a prisoner. She often punished the girl by covering her with a washtub in front of the fireplace. And because she also forced the girl to sweep the ashes out of that chimney, she called her Cindergirl.

The stepmother, determined to expose Cindergirl to peril, said to her one day, "My little one, go to the cave of the fairies to fetch some water. They say the water there is marvelous, that it makes a person younger."

The ever-obedient Cindergirl went to the cave to draw some of the rejuvenating water into a small jar.

"Poor girl, what is it you seek?" asked an old fairy as Cindergirl entered the cavern.

"If you please, godmother, allow me to draw water from your spring."

"Are you in a hurry?" the fairy asked.

"If it would please you, good fairy, I can always tarry a bit," the girl replied.

"Search through my hair, if you would, and see if you can find any fleas or lice."

While Cindergirl was looking through her hair, the fairy asked, "What are you finding in my hair?"

"I'm finding specks of gold and silver."

"You speak correctly, my dear girl. As a reward, whenever you speak, out of your mouth shall come gold, silver, pearls, and beautiful flowers."

And just before she left the cave, Cindergirl was allowed to draw some of the marvelous water.

The step-mother, surprised to see Cindergirl returning, said, "So tell me, have you brought back some rejuvenating water?"

"Yes, the good fairy let me draw from her spring." As she spoke, flowers, pearls, and gold and silver nuggets fell from her lips.

Astonished, the step-mother exclaimed, "I must also send my own daughter to the cave of the fairies."

When the fairy saw the stepmother's daughter arrive, she asked, "My little one, why did you come here?"

"My mother sent me to fetch some of the water that restores youth."

Then, without asking permission, she started drawing water.

"Just wait a bit! Come over here," the old fairy said. "Search through my hair for fleas and lice."

While the girl grimaced and ran her finger's through her hair, the old fairy asked, "What are you finding, child?"

"I'm finding fleas and lice! What do you think!"

Angered by this response, the fairy refused to allow the girl to draw any of the wondrous water and, dismissing her, said, "Whenever you speak, toads and snakes will fall from your mouth."

As soon as the girl returned to the castle, her mother asked, "Have you brought back the rejuvenating water?"

"No, that evil fairy refused to let me have any." As she spoke, toads and snakes fell from her lips.

The very next day, who arrived at the king's castle to court the two princesses? Why, a handsome prince, son of the neighboring king. When he approached the chimney, he sat on the overturned washtub and soon heard faint breathing. He quickly lifted the washtub and discovered Cindergirl. "How beautiful you are!" he exclaimed. "But why are you hiding under this washtub?"

"Because I'm being punished," she replied. As she spoke, flowers, pearls, and gold and silver nuggets fell from her parted lips.

The prince was so taken with her that he instantly proposed marriage. He soon left, promising to return for her the next day in his golden carriage.

The stepmother, seeing him arrive the next day as he'd promised, covered her own daughter's face with a veil and whisked her out the door to the prince's carriage. "It's a long journey," she said to the prince. "My daughter is ready to go."

The girl boarded, and the carriage rolled down the path carrying the princess and the prince. But she spoke along the way, and the carriage soon returned to the castle. The angry prince said to the mother, "Evil woman, you've deceived me. You sent your own daughter instead of Cindergirl, my true fiancée."

He walked to the fireplace and, lifting the washtub, found Cindergirl in tears. He escorted her to his carriage. "You are the one I want to marry," he said.

Happy to see him again, she smiled and spoke; and, marvel of marvels, glittering jewels and flowers streamed from her smiling lips.

Cindergirl and the prince were soon married. And they lived quite happily.

The White Cat
La chatte blanche

Will Ti-Jean, the dreamer who is willing to believe the amazing and fantastic, prevail over his realist, pragmatic, and seemingly more capable brothers?

Once there was a king, and he had three sons. The first was called Cordon-Bleu, or Blue-Cord; the second, Cordon-Vert, or Green-Cord; and the third, Ti-Jean, or Little John.

One day, the king spoke to them. "My sons, you have now come of age. You're strong and hearty, but you don't have much to do. It's time to see if what I've taught you is of any use. You will set out on a journey. He who can find the most beautiful linen will have my crown and my kingdom."

The three young men prepared for their voyage and set out on the king's road. When they reached the place where the road forked in three directions, Cordon-Bleu said "I'll take this path," and Cordon-Vert said, "I'll take this one." Ti-Jean had to be satisfied with the only remaining path. "Well, I'll take this one," he said.

Before going their separate ways, they agreed to meet again in that same place on the Day of St. John's Fires. And off they went. Ti-Jean walked and walked and walked until the road ended at a great forest. He took a path through the trees and kept walking. He soon came upon a cottage with a thatched roof. He stopped, and what an amazing sight he beheld—a large white cat hauling water with four toads the size of donkeys harnessed to a wagon.

"*Pristi!*" said Ti-Jean to himself. And he sat down to watch them work.

The cat, after she'd filled a large tub with water, meowed. "Rrnyow, Rrnyow," she purred and plunged headfirst into the tub. She emerged a princess, beautiful as the dawn, and turned to the young man. "Ti-Jean, what are you searching for?"

"On behalf of my father the king, I'm looking for the most beautiful linen, such as has never been seen in our land. There are three of us, all princes of the kingdom. And our father has promised, by his kingly word, to give his crown to the one among us who brings him the loveliest linen. We three brothers have each taken a different path; but, since they're older, I think the others will probably find more beautiful linen than I will."

"Stay here tonight," she said, "it's too late to return now. In the morning, I will have become a white cat again. But listen closely! Go to my bedchamber and look in the top, left-hand drawer of my bureau. Take the shabbiest of the walnuts you find there and put it in your pocket. When you return to your father, split the walnut with your knife. Then split it and split it and split it again. Out of the walnut will come thirty yards of the most beautiful linen under the sun."

The next morning, Ti-Jean followed the princess's instructions to the letter. When he rejoined his brothers at the fork of the three paths, he saw that they had indeed found some beautiful linen. It fact, between that of Cordon-Bleu and that of Cordon-Vert, it was hard to say which was the most beautiful.

"And how about you, Ti-Jean?" they asked. "You don't seem to have anything."

Ti-Jean said, "Well, Father will certainly have enough linen with what you've brought. He won't want any more than that."

When they arrived, Cordon-Bleu and Cordon-Vert hurried to show the king their beautiful linens. Cordon-Bleu's linen was truly lovely, but that of Cordon-Vert seemed even finer, even silkier. Quite pleased with themselves, the two brothers told their father that Ti-Jean had returned empty-handed.

Then, Ti-Jean appeared, late as usual, pulled the walnut out of his pocket, and handed it to his father. "Here is my old knife, Father. Split this walnut on the corner of the table. Then split it and split it and split it again."

Ti-Jean's brothers laughed aloud. "Look at that dirty walnut. Always the same Ti-Jean, no smarter or dumber than usual."

Then, the king split the walnut. Inside was another walnut.

So he split that one and found another smaller one. Then he kept splitting them, as Ti-Jean had said, until, suddenly, thirty yards of the finest moon-colored linen rolled from the tiniest walnut.

Since it was by far the most beautiful, Ti-Jean had won the contest. His brothers were not happy.

Then the king spoke. "You know that a king has three commands. So there are two more trials for you, my sons."

"What are they, Father?" the young men asked.

"He who brings me the handsomest horse on earth shall have my crown."

The two oldest brothers set out so quickly that Ti-Jean could barely follow. When they reached the fork in the paths, Cordon-Bleu said, "I'm taking the same path, it's the best." Cordon-Vert followed suit and took the path he'd taken the first time. Ti-Jean had little choice and little objection to taking his same path. Before they parted, the brothers had agreed to meet again at that same spot at the waning of the moon.

Ti-Jean walked to the end of the road, followed the path into the forest, and kept walking until he reached the cottage once again. He then sat and watched the white cat hauling water with the toads in harness. The white cat again filled the tub with water. "Rrnyow, Rrnyow," she purred, and again plunged hear first into the tub. And again the cat emerged from the water a princess, even more beautiful that she'd been the first time. Ti-Jean had never seen such a beauty.

And again she asked, "Ti-Jean, what are you looking for?"

"I seek a horse for my father, the king, who has given his second command. The one among us who brings back the handsomest horse will have his crown and kingdom."

"Tomorrow morning, I will again be changed into a white cat," said the princess. "Go then to the stable behind the cottage and take the mangiest of my giant toads. When you reach home, keep that toad in an enclosed place; and, the next morning, he'll be the handsomest horse you've ever seen."

So Ti-Jean followed the princess's instructions. He took the mangiest of the toads, hopped on its back, and rode off. At the fork in the paths, he again met his brothers. And they had indeed brought fine horses!

When they saw Ti-Jean astride the toad, they said, "You'd better not approach our father the king like that. He'll surely kill you!"

But Ti-Jean continued along behind them, urging his mount along.

"This is a disgrace!" exclaimed his brothers. "At least don't follow us so closely."

"Well then," replied Ti-Jean, "move along. What—are you stuck to the road?"

The three brothers arrived at their father's castle quite late, so they stabled their horses. When Ti-Jean ran the currycomb over the frog's back, his brothers said, "Don't do that, you'll ruin Father's currycomb."

"Our father can certainly afford another currycomb," replied Ti-Jean.

The next morning, Cordon-Bleu and Cordon-Vert awoke before daybreak and hurried to show the king their handsome horses.

"What about Ti-Jean?" asked the king.

"Oh, him," the brothers responded, "he brought back a mangy toad."

The king was taken aback. "What? A toad!"

Ti-Jean awoke later than his brothers and went to the stable. His toad had become the handsomest horse on Earth with a glistening, silver mane and shining, golden shoes.

"Aha," said the king, "Ti-Jean has once again prevailed. But you know that I have one more command. He among you who brings back the most beautiful woman in the world will have my crown. This is the final test."

They set out instantly, Cordon-Bleu and Cordon-Vert on their horses, Ti-Jean on his horse. They each took the same path and went on their way. Ti-Jean again came to the cottage in the forest and again saw the white cat. The horse suddenly changed back into a toad. The white cat took her toad back and once again, "Rrnyow, Rrnyow," plunged into the tub of water. She emerged a princess, as beautiful as the moon and radiant as the sun. Ti-Jean fell over backwards, stunned at such beauty. Then, the princess spoke to him.

"This is the third time you've returned. Please tell me what you seek this time, Ti-Jean."

"My father, the king, has given his final command. He who returns with the most beautiful woman in the world will have his crown."

"Oh my, Ti-Jean, that could be a very difficult problem."

"Well, my princess, maybe not so difficult. I've never seen anyone as beautiful as you, nor do I ever expect or want to see such a one."

"But I myself have a very difficult problem to solve, " replied the princess. "An evil old hag cursed me to be a white cat during the day, and I can only regain my human form if the son of a king consents to marry me. I expect to die of loneliness here with my toads and my water tub."

"Wait a minute!" said Ti-Jean. "I'm a prince, the son of a king. Why can't I deliver you from this curse?"

"If that is what, in your heart of hearts, you truly wish to do, I certainly would not say no to you."

"Well, let's go!" exclaimed Ti-Jean.

"Patience, my dear!" replied the princess. "Tomorrow morning, I will again be a white cat. Harness my four toads to the old coach, and together we shall depart."

So the next morning, Ti-Jean harnessed the toads and sat on the coach seat with the white cat by his side. The cat walked across his lap, over his shoulders, and brushed against him affectionately, "Rrnyow, Rrnyow!"

At the fork in the paths, Ti-Jean's brothers waited impatiently. With them were sturdy, pink-cheeked, very beautiful girls. When they saw Ti-Jean approaching with a large white cat, they cried, "Well, this is the living end. He's sure to be drawn and quartered and his parts scattered in four directions!" And they laughed long and loud. "At least do us the favor of not following us with that menagerie of yours," they said.

"Well then," Ti-Jean retorted, "why don't you get moving?"

So he followed his brothers to the castle, urging the toads on with a switch, while the white cat continued to brush against him—"Rrnyow, Rrnyow!"

The next morning, the king saw that Cordon-Bleu and Cordon-Vert indeed had beautiful girls by their sides. He congratulated them and added, "How about Ti-Jean?"

"Oh, he's brought back a huge white cat," they replied.

"Cat or not, by my word as a king, I must see her."

Suddenly, Ti-Jean sprang out of bed. He knew he was late again. He quickly harnessed the four toads, and they changed into the finest horses. Then, in the world's grandest coach, he escorted the princess, beautiful as the dawn and radiant as the sun, to his father.

The king, upon seeing the princess, was completely bedazzled and fell backwards, totally speechless. When he recovered from this shocking though delightful surprise, the king exclaimed, "It is Ti-Jean who has won my kingdom!" And he removed the crown from his own head and put it on Ti-Jean's.

The princess was completely free of the evil hag's curse. And the wedding, a grand and happy occasion if there ever was one, was held the very next day.

The King Makes a Proclamation
Le roi fait battre un ban

✦✦✦✦✦✦✦✦✦✦✦✦✦✦✦

How does the course of true love run? Here Ti-Jean not only has to rescue the princess at great peril to himself, but he also has to undergo intense grilling by the skeptical king, while remaining a dutiful and protective brother to his sister, Jeannette. Note that the "bad guy" at the beginning of the story is the father and not the mother as in "Hansel and Gretel."

Once there lived a gardener and his wife. They were so poor that they had no garden of their own to cultivate. They also had no idea how they would keep feeding their two children, Ti-Jean and Jeannette.

One day, having lost all hope, the gardener said to his wife, "This is impossible, we can't raise these children! We have to take them into the forest and leave them there to fend for themselves."

The mother, moved to the core with tenderness for her children, said, "You can't be thinking of abandoning our children. There has to be another way to resolve this."

"We have two choices," replied the father. "We can watch them die of hunger before our eyes, or we can turn them loose with their own resources. Who knows, they may very well pull themselves through."

The next day, he took the children beyond the mountain, abandoned them, and returned by a roundabout path to his poor cabin.

Ti-Jean and Jeannette found life on their own very difficult. They lived in a cave and ate wild roots and occasionally the birds and small animals that Ti-Jean killed with his bow and arrow. After seven years, Ti-Jean said to his sister, "We've lived here long enough. We're grown up now. Let's look for something else!" So they left.

As darkness fell, they heard wolves howling and feared they'd be devoured in the night. At the edge of the forest, Ti-Jean said, "I'll climb this big tree to see if there are houses nearby." So he climbed the tree and saw a dim light in the distance. He threw his cap to that side to mark the direction and said, "That's the way we have to go."

They walked and walked in the dark through the brush until they arrived at a log house. They could see light flickering from a candle on the table. Three giants, seated on tree stumps, played cards around the table. Something hung from the largest giant's nose and he didn't bother to wipe it away or blow his nose.

"Oh, that makes me sick," said Ti-Jean, "I'll clean his nose off with one of my arrows."

"No, don't be crazy!" Jeannette pleaded. "Those giants eat human flesh. We'll be devoured."

Ti-Jean paid his sister no attention but strung his bow, drew an arrow, aimed through a hole in the corner of the wall, and ZZINNG! He let the arrow fly. The huge card player instantly had a very clean nose.

Furious, the giant turned to his left, and hollered, "Will you stop cleaning my nose like that, since you're such a mucus-face yourself!"

"Not as much of a mucus-face as you are!" his friend replied angrily.

So they went at it, first the two and soon all three of the giants, punching and kicking each other.

"You cleaned off my nose!"

"No, it wasn't me!"

They finally calmed down and started playing cards again. The candle providing light for their game was almost snuffed out by the dripping, hardening gobs of wax, which the giants didn't bother to scrape off. Ti-Jean said to Jeannette, who was crouched by his side in a clump of branches, "I'm going to clean off that candle."

"Don't you dare do something as foolish as that!" said Jeannette. "We could get into big trouble. Didn't you see how they just fought? That was terrifying, the earth shook. If they catch us, they'll swallow us in one bite!"

"I'd just as soon be swallowed whole as starve to death," he retorted; and again he slipped an arrow on his bow string, took aim, and let the arrow fly, cleaning and snuffing the candle right under the noses of the giant card players. In the darkness, the three of them started accusing each other of playing tricks.

"You did that, didn't you?"

"No, I didn't. You snuffed it!"

And thus the fracas began anew. Punches and kicks fell thick and fast, and vicious bites to each other's ears made the giants cry out in agony. Brother and sister felt very small, especially when they saw the furious wildmen coming out of their cabin, romping about until, yes, they discovered the two children. The giants grabbed Ti-Jean and Jeannette by the napes of their necks and carried them off like rabbits into the cabin.

"So you're the one who cleaned my nose, aren't you, you little earthworm!" said the oldest and largest giant.

"Yes I did. That gob hanging from your nose made me sick. You were so busy playing cards that you didn't take care to wipe or blow your nose. So I took care of it for you."

"Did you also take care of the candle, then?" asked the middle giant.

"Yes, the candle was being choked off by the gobs of wax and you were too busy playing cards to clean it. So I did it for you."

"Well, you're pretty handy," said the youngest giant.

And the oldest giant said, "You're not at all timid for one so young. You can give us some urgent help and do us a big favor."

"What favor would that be?" said Ti-Jean.

"On the mountain down there, Princess Nina is being held captive. A small dog with a half-moon on its forehead guards her day and night. To rescue the princess, you must shoot an arrow into that half-moon on the dog's forehead. That's the only way to kill the beast that holds a spell on the captive princess."

"Aiming and shooting arrows is my specialty," said Ti-Jean. "For seven years, we've lived in the forest, and I've had to shoot birds on the fly. I never miss."

"Then you're just the man we need!"

The giants took good care of Ti-Jean and Jeannette. They fed them well—to fatten them up—for as soon as Ti-Jean disposed of the guard dog, the giants planned to eat the two children, fond as they were of eating human flesh. But their immediate plan was to win both the princess and her castle, since the king had promised, "He who rescues her shall marry her."

The next day, the giants led their new-found young friend to the castle where Princess Nina was held captive under the little dog's guard and spell. But there was no way to enter the castle. The doors had been walled up.

The oldest of the giants said, "Ti-Jean, we'll climb on each other's shoulders to provide you a ladder, and you can climb on us to the top floor." Ti-Jean hung his bow over his shoulders and put an arrow between his teeth. He climbed on his "giant ladder" and jumped into the castle through an open window. Then, he saw the little dog who now faced him with its teeth bared. He aimed at the half-moon and let fly. The dog fell to the floor and lay there quite stiff and quite dead.

Ti-Jean ran through the castle until he found Princess Nina's room. She lay in a deep, enchanted sleep. On the round table near her bed, there was a handkerchief, a snuffbox, and a gold ring. Ti-Jean was so taken by Nina's beauty that he fell in love with her on the spot and couldn't help but give her a kiss. As a token, he took the handkerchief and put it in his pocket. He tried in vain to wake her so that he could rescue her. She just slept and slept and slept. He kissed her again and took the snuffbox as a second token. There was nothing he could do to wake Nina, even when he held her tightly, pressed against his wildly beating heart. He kissed her one last time and took the gold ring—a sign of faithfulness—as a final token and put it in his pocket.

Then, he climbed down the living ladder standing at the window and said to the giants, "As long as we leave her in that room in the haunted castle, the princess can't be awakened. The only way to get her out is to dig a hole over there near the basement vent. Then you can follow me in, carry the captive out, and she will awaken."

The oldest of the three giants, who hoped to marry the princess, started digging the hole from the outside with his sword that he then passed to Ti-Jean to finish the work inside.

Ti-Jean said, as he re-entered the castle, "You'd better come through the hole first, Big Giant, followed by you, Medium Giant, and then by you, Little Giant."

When the hole was large enough both outside and in, Big Giant stuffed himself into it head-first. When Big Giant emerged from the hole, but before he stood upright, Ti-

Jean, waiting inside, sliced his head off with one swing of the sword. The second one stuffed himself through, and Ti-Jean greeted him likewise. Same for Little Giant. And that took care of the giants.

Ti-Jean set off by himself to rescue Nina. He carried the princess outside the castle in his arms. As soon as she breathed the fresh air, she awoke, gazed upon her rescuer, and gave him the world's most radiant smile. She loved Ti-Jean as soon as she cast her eyes on him.

Ti-Jean, who always did things properly, set out to return the rescued captive to her father's castle. He left her at the threshold and quietly left to go in search of Jeannette, who had returned to the forest.

Now, the king put forth a second proclamation throughout the kingdom. He who had rescued Nina the princess and also had in his possession, as tokens, her handkerchief, snuffbox, and gold ring, would surely have her hand in marriage. A great feast was already being prepared.

The counts, the barons, and the princes came hastily forward from all parts of the neighboring kingdoms, all hoping to marry Nina. But none could produce the required tokens, and the wedding was delayed. It was put off until the next day, and then to the day after.

"Dear Father," the princess finally said, "you forgot to invite Ti-Jean."

"My dear daughter, he is a mere peasant. I don't want to hear anymore about it!"

"But he's the one who rescued me, and I have proof. With his bow and arrow, he managed to rescue me from the little dog, who was a witch, and from the giants who tried to rescue me and gain my hand."

"My dear girl, what can I do?"

"Send for Ti-Jean!" she said.

But Ti-Jean could not be found anywhere. He had returned to the forest to hunt rabbits and take care of Jeannette.

The king, in a sour mood because Nina wouldn't even consider the barons and princes, put forth yet another proclamation to the four corners of the kingdom, even to the edge of the dark forest. Ti-Jean, encouraged by his sister, finally responded to the king's order. Upon entering the castle, where the banquet celebration languished, he was led to the seat of honor at Princess Nina's side. She held her arms out to him in expectation. Then the king confronted the new arrival. "Are you really the one who rescued the princess? Tell me how it happened! I want all the details," he demanded.

"When I entered her room, she was sleeping," Ti-Jean began.

"Did you at least wake her up?"

"No, I only took her handkerchief from the round table near her bed."

"Well, you're quite a rescuer of princesses!" said the king peevishly.

"I put the handkerchief in my pocket," Ti-Jean continued hesitantly. "Then, I allowed myself a small liberty that I can't possibly mention in front of all these people."

"Proof, give me proof!" cried the king, more agitated than ever.

"Here it is!" replied Ti-Jean, pulling the handkerchief out of his pocket.

"A handkerchief," retorted the king, "can easily be stolen while passing near a table. The princess was asleep."

"On the table, there was a snuffbox," Ti-Jean countered. "I took it and put it in my pocket."

"Proof, give me proof!" cried the king, twice as angry.

"Here it is," said Ti-Jean as he pulled the snuffbox out of his pocket. "Then I allowed myself another tiny liberty that I wouldn't dare speak of in front of all these people."

"A snuffbox can easily be stolen as one passes by a table. The princess was sleeping," sneered the king.

Ti-Jean, nudged in the ribs by Nina and losing patience with the king, pressed on. "There, on the round table, was a gold ring. I took it and put it in my pocket. Here it is!"

He put the ring on the table in front of his beloved Nina, who immediately slipped it on her finger. The ring fit her as perfectly as on the day of her capture. She turned to Ti-Jean, who had so bravely rescued her from the dog and giants. She held out her arms and kissed him unblushingly, as he had kissed her during her bewitched slumber, a kiss of true love.

The people and the king, delighted by this revelation, began applauding and praising Ti-Jean. By the king's word, and in all justice, it was only fitting that Nina wed the rescuer, her hero.

Franco-American— and We Don't Mean Spaghetti

These are stories just for the sake of telling stories and to celebrate people's strengths while lightening their burdens by laughing at their weaknesses and peculiarities. These tales are often told around the kitchen table or on the front porch. A keen listener learns from these what qualities people admire, what is worthy of scorn, and what kind of wisdom is valued on a daily basis. Life may sometimes be a strange and difficult trip, but it's a lot more fun if we can laugh at the unexpected turns and at ourselves as we careen into and out of those curves.

Pierre and the Chain Saw
Pierre et la tronçonneuse

✢ ✢ ✢ ✢ ✢ ✢ ✢ ✢ ✢ ✢ ✢ ✢ ✢ ✢ ✢ ✢

Both French-Canadians and Franco-Americans have been the butt of various ethnic jokes. Tales depicting the "Dumb Frenchman" are still told in the Northeast, sometimes even by people who reluctantly admit their own French origins. "Pierre and the Chain Saw" is an example of a joke that is not simply a one-sided ethnic slur. In this case Pierre is the butt of the joke but not because of innate stupidity. The story chuckles at Pierre's isolation and backwardness while it celebrates his prowess as a woodsman. Why, Pierre and his old hand saw just might be able to keep up with someone using a modern chain saw!

*ll the woodcutters in the great woods of Québec and northern Maine spoke highly of Pierre Bergeron's abilities. He could cut, split, and stack more than four cords of wood in a single day.

Though Pierre was well-known and well-liked, he seldom went into town. He was happy living with his wife, Marie, and their nine children in the deep woods, where they always graciously received the few visitors who came to their door.

One day Pierre's old chum, André Labranche, came to visit. They talked, told stories, and shared the latest news as they smoked their pipes and drank some of Marie's fine coffee. Suddenly, André turned to Pierre.

"Oh, my friend, I almost forgot to tell you about a brand new in-ven-tion that's gonna make it so we can cut twice as much wood."

"Oh yeah! And what is it called, this in-ven-tion?"

"It is called a 'chain saw,' and they got some at the hardware store in town for one hundred dollars."

"So André, have you tried this chain saw, or have you not tried this chain saw?"

"I don't have one hundred dollars!"

"Well, maybe I can find one hundred dollars. But a saw that can cut more than the one I've been using for twenty-three years, I don't think I can find that at the hardware store. No, I don't think so."

In the weeks following André's visit, Pierre thought about the new invention and talked to Marie about it. Finally, Marie said, "Pierre, my husband, when next time you go to town, put your eyes on this chain saw and see what you think!"

So he did. He went into the hardware store and asked Monsieur Gauthier to show him the new invention. The proprietor pointed to the rack where a dozen gleaming red chain saws were displayed. Pierre inspected the saws closely then approached the counter with one.

"This thing is pretty as a picture, but how do I know if it can cut twice as much wood as my old saw?"

"Oh, it's guaranteed," said Mr. Gauthier. "We have had good reports about it."

"So if it does not do twice the cutting, what happens?"

"You bring it back with the receipt, and I give you your money back!"

"Hokay!" Pierre said and slapped down five twenty dollar bills and eagerly headed home with his new invention.

About three days later, Monsieur Gauthier was surprised to see Pierre burst through the door, chain saw and receipt in hand. "Give me my one hundred dollars back, Gauthier! This thing is no good! I been working like a beaver for three days and can barely cut as much wood with this chain saw as I can with my good old saw!"

"Well, Pierre, I'm very sorry to hear that," said Mr. Gauthier. "Here's your money back."

Pierre handed over the chain saw, slapped the receipt on the counter, grabbed his money and started out the door. Monsieur Gauthier, curious as to what the problem might be, pulled the starter-cord. The chain saw sputtered and roared.

Pierre, startled, turned in the doorway. "My God, Gauthier, what is that noise?"

The Shoemaker and the Spinner

Le cordonnier et la fileuse

This tale is actually two stories more or less linked by a festive meal. In the first, the local king appears to be an accessible, folksy type who is nevertheless oblivious to the woes of his people, and at least two of the villagers are enterprising souls. The second tale picks up with the battle of the sexes, with each gender taking its share of the blows.

*O*n old shoemaker and his wife, an old spinner, were living their last years in a tiny cottage, ten feet by twelve, at the end of a village that had become deserted. They had once known good times and had had enough work; now, even despite the bad times, they had maintained a love of labor and their good humor. They sang away, he keeping time with his foot, she, with her spinning wheel or loom.

But one day, there was no work at all. There were those who advised, "Good people, do like everyone else, and leave this place. Go somewhere else!"

And the old couple responded, "We have lived in this place; we'll die here."

Closing the door, the old man muttered, "In his skin the toad will die!" But lacking money, they soon had nothing left to eat. Beset by hunger the shoemaker said to his wife, "It seems that the king has need of a shoemaker. I am old, but the king is a good man. He will surely have pity on me and give me a little work. Old woman, if you are willing, we will go, tomorrow, to seek him out."

For her part, the spinner was not about to say no.

The next day they set out; and, because they traveled slowly, it took them until nightfall to reach the king's castle. They knocked on the huge, oaken door, and a porter opened it for them.

"Sir," said the porter, "what can I do for you?"

"We want to see his highness the king." The porter went off to get the king.

"Well, good evening, monsieur. Good evening, madame!" said the king. "Is it the good weather that brings you?"

"Good weather," responded the shoemaker, "is less lacking for us than work."

"Work?" asked the king, surprised, because he lacked of nothing.

The old man explained, "I am a shoemaker, a good shoemaker. My old wife, here, is a spinner and a weaver, but we have nothing to do. We now face misery. If you do not have pity on us, we will die of hunger. Do you have work for us?"

Truly saddened, the king answered, "Right now I have enough people at my service." Then he added, "But two more or less are not going to make any difference. Tonight, you will sleep at the castle; and tomorrow, you, shoemaker, will begin to make shoes for each of my servants, and you, spinner, will knit as many pairs of socks.

It goes without saying that the shoemaker and the spinner agreed.

"Measure the feet of my thirty servants," added the king as he departed.

The next day, the old man and his wife went right to work. Soon they were singing again, he keeping time with his foot, and she with the spinning wheel or her knitting needles. By the time the project was completed, they had accumulated quite a profit.

Happy as in the good old days, they returned to their cottage with the thought of having a feast. The spinner said to her husband, "Go buy some flour so I can make *crêpes.*"

"But you don't have a frying pan," said he.

"Husband, don't get upset for so little a thing. Just go out and borrow one!"

The shoemaker bought a bag of flour. Passing by a neighbor's house on the way, he borrowed a frying pan with a long handle. Back home, he sat on his stool and began cutting leather and keeping time with his foot, while his wife mixed the flour and got to work frying *crêpes.*

"The *crêpes* are all fried," called the old woman. "Come eat!"

The old man sat himself down at the table as did the old woman, and they ate *crêpes.* And more *crêpes!* They were delicious! Not in a long time had the couple so filled their stomachs. At the end, a few *crêpes* were left; but husband and wife were so full, they couldn't even touch them with a fork.

When the meal was over, they thought about the borrowed frying pan. The spinner said, "Husband, go take the frying pan back; I have to wash the dishes."

The shoemaker, who was not in a hurry, answered, "I went to get it. Now it's your turn to take it back."

"You will return it!" insisted the old woman.

"It's not my job to take it back," said he.

"You're not being reasonable. Go on!

"It's your turn to go."

"You are the one who will go!"

"Me? I refuse to go!"

So there they were again, going on and on—just like in the old days.

"Get going!"

"To heck with you!"

The spinner was out of answers, so she said to the shoemaker, "Let's make a deal. You are always saying that women talk a lot ..."

"Yup, I say it and I repeat it now: women have a loose tongue ..."

"Well, let's just see!" said his wife. "The first one to talk will return the frying pan. Understood?"

"It's a deal!"

Satisfied, the shoemaker picked up his leather and thread and returned to work. He put the shoe between his knees, adjusted the sole, wet the thread with saliva, threaded the needle, pushed the needle, pulled the strand, and banged the hammer. Zip, pee, pan, pan! Meanwhile, the spinner selected the strands of carded wool and began to push the pedal up and down. Soon the wheel was humming, and the wool was spinning right along.

As he cut the leather and tapped his foot, the shoemaker's song kept rhythm with the movement:

Tou-lou-lou-lou-lou-loum
Tou-lou-lou-lou-loum
Tou-de-loutâ-dl-lou tâ-dl-lou-loum
Tou-lou-lou-lou-loum
Tou-lou-lou-lou-lou-loum
To-de-lou tâ-dl-lou-tâ-dl-lou-loum ...

Twisting the wool with the end of her fingers, the spinner was also singing without words, but out on a totally different melody. Her voice was high and had a nasal quality:

Ta-dl-la-dl-la
Ta-dl-la-dl-la

174

Ta-dl-la ta-dl-la-ta-dl-la-ta
Ta-dl-la-dl-la
Ta-dl-la-dl-la
Ta-ta-dl-la-dl-la
Ta-dl-la ta-dl-la ta-dl-la ...

Suddenly, tap, tap, tap, someone was knocking on the door. What to do? Neither the shoemaker nor the spinner could say, "Come in!" The visitor knocked again, a little louder this time, as though to say, "Come on, people of this house!"

But the couple went on singing without stirring an inch. The door opened; and the stranger, without further ado, simply invited himself in. Throwing a simple glance his way, the shoemaker and the spinner continued foot tapping, wool twisting and singing, *Tou-lou-lou-loum* and *Ta-dl-la-dl-la* ...

Now that he was in the house, the stranger yelled out, "Good day to you, monsieur shoemaker! Good day to you, madame spinner!"

The old man and his wife did not reply but went on singing their tunes. The situation made little sense.

"Sir," asked the stranger, "am I far from the Fifth Row of Poverty-Place?"

Somewhat embarrassed, the shoemaker wet his thread, pushed it into the needle, and into the sole. He glanced over at his wife, but she hadn't budged. With no answer, he sang away: *Tou-lou-lou-lou-loum!*

"Sir, speak up!" pleaded the newcomer, still louder. "How far from here to Poverty-Place?"

No answer! Nothing but *Tou-lou-lou* ... and *Ta-dl-la* ...

"Are these people deaf, or are they crazy enough to be tied up? I'll find out ..."

Turning to the spinner, the stranger asked, "Madame, how far is it, by way of the King's Road, from your house to Poverty-Place Row?"

175

A renewed *ta-dl-la dl-la* ... was her only answer, and the string of wool got longer and longer in the spinner's fingers.

"My dear lady," said the visitor, coming a little closer now, "you are no longer in your twenties, but I find you a fresh as a beautiful apple. I would very much like to look at you up close."

Surprised, the shoemaker dropped his needle and thread and stared at the intruder.

"Madame, would you oblige a passer-by who desires a little favor?"

The shoemaker's hammer dropped to the floor and the *tou-lou-lou-lou-loum* lost much of its enthusiasm. For his part, the questioner was gaining ground in an enterprise that was fast becoming flirtatious.

"Madame, for your age, you do not lack grace. They'd told me that the women of Poverty-Place were the most good-looking of the canton, and I wanted to see for myself."

With his finger, he caressed the spinner's chin. She got up and backed away. Stunned, the shoemaker dropped his shoe and ran his hand through his hair that now stood on his head like the quills of a porcupine. From the depths of his throat, he growled out his tune. *Tou-lou-lou-lou-loum* had now became a warning.

"Madame, madame, ah! be more indulgent to me!"

Retreating another step before the insolent stranger, she found herself backing against the wall. Pleading, she raised her hand to the sound of *Ta-dl-la-dl-la* ...!

"Madame, I can resist no longer," said the stranger, pretending to kiss the woman.

"Leave her alone!" the furious shoemaker cried out, ready to strike the aggressor.

The old spinner burst out laughing; and, pointing to her husband, she yelled, "You spoke first. Go bring back the frying pan!"

They always say that women possess loose tongues. Well, go tell that to the old shoemaker of Poverty Place. He never again made that comment to his wife.

Montréal Hockey
Le hockey à Montréal

✦✦✦✦✦✦✦✦✦✦✦✦✦✦✦✦✦

Hockey has long been an obsession of Canadians in general and of French-Canadians in particular. The Forum, where the Montreal Canadians have won numerous National Hockey League Championships, is considered a shrine in the minds and hearts of loyal and rabid fans. Since most of the players were French-Canadians, the team was a source of great ethnic pride. (M.P.)

*T*wo French-Canadians met on the street.

"Oh, Pierre," said the first, "what a dream I had last night. I was playing for the Canadiens! It was the seventh game of the Stanley Cup. We're in the third sudden-death overtime. I get the puck. I fly down the ice. I maneuver that puck around everybody with my great stick-handling. I pull the goalie out of the net with a great fake. I put a backhand behind him. I am the toast of Montréal. The players carry me around the ice. The crowd cheers!"

"Oh, Claude, I had a dream last night, too," said Pierre.

"I dreamed I'm staying in one of the big suites at the Queen Elizabeth Hotel. In the middle of the night I hear a knock on my door. I open the door and who is standing there? Brigitte Bardot. And standing right next to her is Raquel Welch."

"You mean to say," Claude exclaimed, "that you had those two beautiful women right there and you didn't call me!"

"Oh, I called you, all right," Pierre replied, "but they told me you were at the Forum playing hockey."

Cricket the Smartest Figure-Outer

Criquette fin devineur par-dessus fin devineur

In 1968, two brothers in Augusta, Maine, Émile—the younger—and Arthur Lévesque, each told this story in slightly different versions to their niece, Claire Violette. They had heard it from their father, Ferdinand Lévesque. Claire transcribed both versions and placed them in the Archives of Folklore and Oral History at the University of Maine in Orono, where I found them in the mid-1970s. I combined the two versions into one story, adding my own tidbits and adapting it to my audiences. Then, in 1995, I had the pleasure of visiting with Émile Lévesque, now ninety-one, and hearing him tell "Cricket the Smartest Figure-Outer" himself. (J.O.)

Cricket was lazy. In fact, he was perhaps the laziest guy around. He just didn't want to work and claimed that he could make a living just by being smart. One day, he left his mother and his village, setting out to make his fortune in the city.

Along the way he met a fortune teller and decided this profession was indeed the way to make a lot of money. Cricket could not tell the future, but he could figure things out. He made a sign and slipped it over his head so that it

hung in front and back. Each side read: *Fin devineur par-
dessus fin devineur*—The smartest figure-outer of them all.

But business wasn't very good. Occasionally, he met
people who asked him questions, and Cricket usually
came up with pretty good answers. A very moral person,
Cricket made it a point never to lie. A person might say,
"Is it going to be nice?" Thinking very hard, Cricket would
say, "Yes, yes indeed, it is going to be very nice." Or, "No,
no, it won't be nice at all." Of course, most kinds of weather
are nice for some but not for all. A farmer might want rain;
and a bride, beautiful sunshine. All in all, he answered the
questions, but this did not seem to be a successful way to
get rich.

One day, when Cricket had eaten nothing but one
hard crust of bread in eight days, he passed beneath the
balcony of a palace. The king, whose vision was poor, said
to a servant, "What do the signs say on that man?"

"Why, your majesty, they read: The smartest figure-
outer of them all."

"Well go down right now and get that man. Bring him
to me," demanded the king.

The servant ran down and grabbed Cricket, giving
him no chance at all to refuse. "The king wants to see you!"
he announced.

Cricket was a sad sight, coming before the king in his
dirty clothes. "What does your sign say?" asked the king.

"It says, uh, that I am the greatest person in the world
for figuring things out."

"Are you some sort of a magician?" asked the king.
"If you're lying, I'll have you put to death!"

Oh, oh, Cricket thought, now you've had it. You've
overstepped yourself. Maybe you should have stayed
home. But you can't back down now; it's too late.

"Yes, indeed, your majesty, I can figure anything out,"
he said rather timidly.

"Okay," the king said. "Here's the story. Look at my daughter over there. She cries night and day. There is no consoling her. And I can't take much more of this! The princess had a very valuable engagement ring, and one day she lost it. Now she cries all the time. You will find it. If you do, I will give you a fine salary and an excellent reward too. If you fail, I will feed you to the lion in that cage over there! You have three days."

Cricket, always ready to make the best of a bad situation, decided that he could at least enjoy those last three days. "Sire, for this job, I will need a lot of strength. You must feed me whatever I request."

"It shall be so," responded the king. "You can feast every day for three days. All you have to do is tell these three servants what you want," he added, pointing to the men. "They are charged with caring for your needs; but they will also be your guards so don't try to escape!"

As Cricket passed the lion, the animal, who had not eaten all day, let out a mighty roar. Cricket decided then and there that he did not like the lion.

Of course, Cricket, dirty as he was, did not eat with the king. He was assigned to the servants' quarters. When dinner time approached, he ordered the biggest and best meal he could think of. The servants prepared the food and took it to him, and then they stood guard. When he finished, Cricket pushed himself away from the table. Remembering that his days were numbered, he said aloud, "Well, there's the first one!"

On hearing these words, the servants became uneasy. "What's he talking about?" they wondered among themselves. "Do you think he knows?" asked the first. "Impossible," said the second. "Quiet, fools!" warned the third.

Why were the servants nervous?

A short time ago, the princess had removed her ring at the table to show it off and had then left it on the tablecloth. The servants, who shook the leftovers into the lion's cage, had found the ring and decided to keep it.

On the second day, Cricket ordered another feast. The servants watched closely. When he finished, Cricket pushed away from the table and said out loud, "Well, there's the second one!"

"That's it!" said the first servant."He's figured everything out!"

"Better confess and hope for the best," said the second.

"Quiet, fools!" warned the third.

On the third and last day, Cricket could hardly figure out what to order. He asked the servants for advice. They could have given him something very bad—like poison—but these men were only thieves, not murderers. They prepared the grandest meal of all, hoping it would be Cricket's last. When Cricket finished, he pushed himself away from the table and said, "Well, there's the third!"

"He's figured it out!" said the three servants, and they ran up to Cricket.

"We didn't mean anything wrong!" said the first.

"We really only found it ourselves!" said the second.

"You won't tell, will you!" implored the third.

Well, this *is* an interesting development, thought Cricket. "No, I won't give you away," he answered; "but you must hand over the ring right now." And they did.

Cricket, however, was now stuck with the ring. He couldn't just give it to the king, who would want to know where he found it. He went for a walk to think things over. Passing in front of the lion's cage, he shuddered to think what could have become of him. The lion blared a gigantic roar, and Cricket got an idea. The next time the lion opened his mouth, Cricket threw in the ring. Down it went to where he hoped the ring would stay for a while.

The next morning, the king summoned Cricket. "Hey, I told you three days. You're overdue. Where's my daughter's ring?"

"Oh that? I don't have it, but I know where it is."

"Don't fool with me, young man! I'll throw you to the lion. Where is it?"

"Well, you just said it, Sire. The lion has it. I guess you'll have to cut open the lion to find the ring."

"What! My favorite lion, worth thousands of dollars?" said the king in disbelief.

"Well, it's up to you," Cricket said coolly. "It's either the lion or the ring. You'll find it inside."

"You'd better not be wrong," the king threatened as he dispatched the servants to retrieve his shotgun and knives. So the men killed the lion. But they did not find the ring in the lion's stomach nor did they find it in the small intestine. They did discover it, however, in the large intestine. The first servant, the second servant, the third servant, and Cricket all sighed quietly.

The princess cried out for joy. Despite his loss, the king was overjoyed at seeing the princess happy, because he could not have taken much more of her crying. The king, a man of his word, paid Cricket his salary in gold and added a handsome reward too.

Cricket was anxious to go home. He would show his mother how smart he really was. Holding his bags of gold, he headed out of the palace and across the courtyard. A servant girl swept the stones, and she caught a cricket under her broom. "Hey," she said, "aren't you the guy who's supposed to be able to figure everything out? I think you're a fake. If you're so smart, tell me what I've got under my broom. Tell me the truth, or I'll turn you in!"

"Poor Cricket. This time you've had it!" Cricket said.

"Why, you are good!" the astonished girl admitted.

And Cricket went on his way.

D'Amours the Fastest Runner in the World
Le D'Amours qui courait tant

✦✦✦✦✦✦✦✦✦✦✦✦✦✦✦✦✦

This is another story from the "Lévesque Repertoire" that I'd been telling and retelling, both in French and English, since the mid-1970s and finally got to hear in 1995 in Augusta, Maine, from Émile Lévesque himself. I can't hold Mr. Lévesque accountable for the variations I have included over the years! (J.O.)

*B*ack in Canada, years ago, there lived a man named D'Amours, and he had the reputation for being a fantastic runner.

At the same time, there was a man around Trois-Pistoles who owned some sheep. Although his name was Médore Rioux, they called him Père, or Father Médore. Père Médore had put his sheep in the north pasture for the summer. Sheep are funny; if they aren't looked after, they become wild. They can't just be left alone all summer. Père Médore didn't care to look after those sheep, and he didn't feel like going up into the mountain country. He told himself he didn't have time, that he had too much other work to do, that he was all alone to take care of everything on the farm ... Anything to keep from having to go up there!

Fall came along and soon the first snowfall. Père Médore said to himself, I suppose I'd better go up and get those sheep! So he nudged himself up into the north pasture where he expected to gather his flock. But the sheep were nowhere to be seen. After looking for a while, he finally spotted one. Zip! Off she went as if the Devil was after her. Père Médore spotted a few more, but they always bolted off quicker than he could catch them. Those critters were more like deer than sheep!

So the next day, Père Médore returned with a couple of men. They tried to round up the sheep. Nothing doing! Père Médore said to himself, I'll either have to forget those sheep or shoot 'em. And he headed back home.

During the week, Père Médore heard about a man in the village of Trois-Pistoles by the name of D'Amours. Remember, this man had the reputation as a fast runner. "He brags a lot, but he's good," people said. So after mass on Sunday, Père Médore went off to find the famous D'Amours. When he located him, Père Médore told D'Amours his problem. "What do you think?" asked the older man.

"*Aiyoille*, Père!" answered D'Amours. "Sure I can catch those sheep for you. But it's gonna cost you fifty cents a head."

In those days fifty cents was a lot of money. In fact, one living, breathing sheep cost only four dollars! Père Médore tried bargaining, but nothing doing.

"Take it or leave it!" said D'Amours.

Better to lose fifty cents than four dollars, thought Père Médore, and the bargain was struck. Twenty sheep at fifty cents a head.

They headed up the mountain. By afternoon they had reached the pasture. "This is the place," said Père Médore.

"OK," nodded D'Amours. "But I'm not gonna worry about those sheep today. Tomorrow. Yup, tomorrow morning, I'll fetch 'em for you." So they went to the cabin. Later, the two men spent the evening in the light of a kerosene lantern playing cards and checkers. They stayed up most of the night, and Médore thought that D'Amours would get a late start on Monday.

In fact, by the time Père Médore woke up the next morning, D'Amours was gone. "He'll never get them!" said Médore as he made himself breakfast. In fact, he almost hoped that the runner would not succeed. "Brags too much for his own good. It'll almost be worth losing the sheep just to show him up," smiled the owner.

Night came and still there was no D'Amours. Père Médore decided to go to bed. "Maybe he got himself lost, or he gave up and went home!" he chuckled. Just then a big clatter erupted out by the pen. Pére Médore lit the lantern and ran out to see what was going on. D'Amours came out of the barn with his clothes torn. He was scratched and disheveled. In the barn the animals made a lot of noise. Père Médore yelled to make himself heard, "How did it go?"

"Nothing to it," D'Amours yelled back.

"How did you manage to get them?" asked the older man.

"Pretty easy, at least for the big ones."

"The big ones? What do you mean, the big ones? They were all big," said Père Médore. "Maybe they had lambs?" He went to the barn to see for himself.

In the barn were twenty sheep and ... twenty rabbits. "Those little ones can sure run," said D'Amours.

After that, nobody cared how much D'Amours bragged about being the fastest runner. They knew it was true.

GLOSSARY

- *Aiyoille:* An exclamation; the equivalent of Ai!

- *Allô:* Hello (informal).

- *Allons-y:* Let's go.

- *Arpent:* An old French measurement, roughly an acre.

- *Aux États:* Lit., to the United States.

- *Bonjour:* Good day; hello or good-bye.

- *Canuck:* Derogatory nickname for French-Canadians and Franco-Americans.

- *Chanter la guignolée:* A tradition of extending good wishes to neighbors with group singing—similar to Christmas caroling.

- *Chantier:* Any work area; here, in the forest.

- *Chasse-galerie:* Lit., chase porch; origin uncertain; perhaps *porch* represents home, and *chase* is its pursuit.

- *Chez nous:* Lit., at us; at our place, home.

- *Cocorico:* As all French-speaking roosters crow.

- *Cotillon:* Cotillion; a dance.

- *Confitures:* Fruit preserves.

- *Contrecoeur:* Lit., against the heart or against one's will; a town.

- *Coureurs-de-bois:* Runners of the woods; the unlicensed French trapper-explorers in seventeenth and eighteenth century North America.

- *Crêpe:* Thin French pancake made of milk, flower, eggs, and a little oil.

- *Crête:* Lit., crest; an unusual family name.

- *Creton:* A meat spread made from pork. It has linguistic variations, such as groton and guerton.

- *Devineur:* Diviner, magician; more like figure-outer.

- *Dîner:* Dinner; always the noon-day meal.

- *Écu:* Lit., shield; here, an ancient gold coin.

- *Guignolée:* Collection for the poor; singing that should result in donations; here, similiar to "going caroling."

- *Habitant:* An inhabitant; a farmer.

- *Jean:* John.

- *L'Avenir National:* Lit., *The National Future*; daily French-language newspaper published from 1894-1949 in Manchester, New Hampshire.

- *Le bon:* The good.

- *Le diamant:* Diamond.

- *Le lecondaire:* Temperance League.

- *Le jour de l'an:* Lit., the day of the year; New Year's Day.

- *Lieue:* League; ancient measure equaling about 2.5 miles.

- *Louisiane:* Louisiana.

- *Memère:* Grandmother.

- *Métis:* A person of "mixed" Native American and European ancestry.

- *Mon oncle:* My uncle; also, uncle.

- *Monsieur:* Lit., my sire; Mister.

- *Noël:* Christmas; a common enough first name among men.

- *Oui:* Yes.

- *Pepère:* Grandfather.

- *Père:* Father; also an official title for priests and a title of respect for older men.

- *Petit-Canada:* Little Canada; French-Canadian section of town in the United States.

- *Petite-Misère:* Lit., Little Misery; a town.

- *Pistole:* An ancient gold coin

- *Pristi:* An exclamation about equivalent to *dammit.*

- *Raconteur:* Storyteller.

- *Rigodon:* Rigaudon or rigadoon, a dance of the seventeenth and eighteenth century in double meter; here, a dance party.

- *Seigneurie:* A system in feudal times in which a lord owned all the land while the peasants worked the field and brought in the crops. In exchange, the lord protected and governed the workers, who were allowed to keep a subsistence portion of that crop.

- *Soirées de rire:* Lit., evening of laughter, where stories were told and songs were sung.

- *Ti-Jean:* Lil' (Little) John.

- *Tonnerre!:* Thunder!; used as an exclamation.

- *Voyageurs:* Travelers; the licenced French traveler-explorers in seventeeth and eighteenth century North America.

Notes

✦✦✦✦✦✦✦✦✦✦✦✦✦✦✦

Ti-Jean Dry Bread

Translated and adapted from a story told by Joseph Patry of the Beauce region in Québec in 1913, this story was collected by Marius Barbeau and published in *Grand-mère Raconte* (*Grandmother Tells Stories*) (Montréal: Éditions Beauchemin, 1935).

Ti-Jean is an abbreviation for Petit-Jean, literally, Little John. The character, Ti-Jean, is a central figure in the French-Canadian folk tradition, as well as in the folklore of other French-speaking peoples. In Louisiana, for example, he is Jean-Sot, or Crazy John. Ti-Jean is also very similar to "Jack," the well-known, omnipresent character in tales of the English-speaking world. He is a kind of "Everyman," who is presented as clever and resourceful in many tales and as a somewhat helpless dolt in others. When people heard these tales throughout the centuries, they likely looked around their social circles and inside themselves and recognized many of the positive and negative characteristics displayed by Ti-Jean.

For a whole book of Ti-Jean stories, see Melvin Gallant's *Ti-Jean, Contes acadiens* (Acadian Tales) (Moncton, N.B.: Éditions d'Acadie, 1984), or *Fools and Rascals* by Calvin André Claudel (Lafayette, La.: Legacy Publishing Co., 1978).

In the original story, Ti-Jean slices the heads off the three giants. With some trepidation, Michael made the change that both incapacitates the giants and displays Ti-Jean's ingenuity. It's quite likely that various changes were gradually introduced into these stories through the years as they passed from teller to teller. Each of the tellers probably felt the same reluctance to change the received version as he or she also walked that thin line between being faithful to the previous tellings and adapting the story to their own times and their own audiences.

Variations of this story can be found in Jack tales, including "Jack the Giant Killer," "A Thousand at a Blow," in a Spanish tale, "Don Juan Calderon Kills Seven," and in various European versions like "The Little Tailor."

Uncle Noël's Story

Told to Julien in the mid-1970s by his uncle, Noël Boisvert, Julien then published it in *D'la boucane* (Cambridge, Mass.: National Assessment and Dissemination Center, 1979).

Note that not all people flooding into New England from Canada during the manufacturing boom of the nineteenth and early twentieth centuries settled in mill towns. Concord was the state capital, upstream on the Merrimack River from world-famous Manchester. It offered available farmland but no real industrial jobs.

Boisvert literally means "greenwood." In the process of immigrating to the United States, many Boisverts became Greenwoods.

The Split Boulder

Translated, with some retelling, from Andrée Lebailly's story *Le caillou coupé* found in *Les Contes du Chalin aux îls Saint-Pierre et Miquelon* (Ottawa: Les Éditions Leméac Inc., 1984), this story is told with the gracious permission from the author and publisher.

"The Split Boulder" begins in France, in the town of Avranches, located on the southern end of the Cherbourg peninsula before Normandy gives place to Brittany. This ancient town is a neighbor to the famous Mont-Saint-Michel and was the sight of a blistering battle led by the United States tanks in 1944. The legend finishes on the French island of Saint Pierre—of bootlegging fame during the Prohibition Era.

The lightning on the islands is said by the inhabitants to have a magical quality. They have given it the name *le chalin*.

Ti-Jean Joins the Elite

This story was adapted and expanded from a story told to Michael by Ron Evans.

Ron Evans is a storyteller and "Keeper of the Talking Stick" for his own people, the Chippewa-Cree *Métis* settlement in Northern Saskatchewan. He has traveled throughout the world as a performer and teacher of his people's unique stories.

Since part of Ron's heritage is French-Canadian, he is familiar with the Ti-Jean stories. In the early 1980s, he told Michael two of them—"Ti-Jean Joins the Elite," and "Ti-Jean, Mama, and the Landlord." Both tales reflect attitudes and biases quite typical of many French-Canadians. Michael hasn't found either of these stories in print. So almost fifteen years later, he has depended on his memory and a scribbled outline to create these versions. Thus, he takes full responsibility for the significant changes and additions to Ron's originals.

Deception through doctoring and other trickery is a common folktale motif. For example, see "Cricket, the Smartest Figure-Outter," in this collection, a clever deception to gain riches. The German folktale hero Tyll Eulenspiegel (also known as Tyl or Till), pulls a trick similiar to Ti-Jean's in order to earn a fee of five hundred gulden.

My Grandfather the Magician
Julien's mother, Alice Lacasse Olivier, told him this family story. It can also be found in *Amoskeag* by Tamara K. Hareven (New York: Pantheon Books, 1968).

Amoskeag, in Penacook Indian dialect, means "abundance of fish." The Amoskeag Falls in Manchester were both a favorite fishing site and a sacred place for Native Americans of the area.

The Amoskeag Mills were at the heart of Manchester's phenomenal nineteenth century growth, becoming "the largest textile mill yard in the world." In 1912, for example, the mile-long, multiple-story mills employed 15,500 persons and produced fifty miles of cloth *every* hour. See, among others, *The Merrimack Valley, New Hampshire* by Gary Samson (Norfolk, Va.: The Donning Co., 1989).

The Corporations were the housing provided to the workers by the Amoskeag Manufacturing Company. Rent was nominal—a few dollars a month—and subletting was allowed. Moreover, besides serving her own large family, Julien's grandmother Lacasse cooked meals for the workmen.

Bénissez-nous, Seigneur ...: Bless us, O Lord ... The traditional blessing before the meal was *de rigueur* in Franco-American families.

The Handsome Dancer
Translated and adapted from a story told by J.E.A. Cloutier of Cap St-Ignace, it was collected and published in *L'arbre des rêves* (The Tree of Dreams) (Montréal: Les Éditions Lumen, 1947).

The Temperance League (*Le Lacondaire*) was a social organization sponsored by the parish churches. Its members were dedicated to avoiding alcohol consumption. A black cross was given to families who took the pledge.

According to collector Marius Barbeau, many versions of this legend have been collected, this one appearing in print as early as 1837. This story is sometimes called "Rose Latulippe."

The *Loup-Garou*

This story was translated and adapted from *Le Terroir*, page 247, a document labeled A-40 in the Archives de Folklore of the Université Laval; Ste-Foy, Québec.

Many werewolf stories exist throughout the word. What seems distinctive about this one, and French-Canadian *loup-garou* tales in general, is the strong connection to religious beliefs. Note that in this story, the setting, ironically, is in the town of Beauséjour, which literally means "pleasant visit."

In her collection *Favorite Folktales from Around the World*, Jane Yolen offers a variant called "The Cat Woman." The French story is widely known, and Yolen point out that it ends with the motif, "Cat's paw cut off, woman's hand missing."

In the book, *L'arbre des Rêves* (Tree of Dreams) by Marius Barbeau, reference is made to a man who was said to have inhabited a cow. Thus, it was that people could be condemned to becoming "werepigs" and "werecows" as well as werewolves.

For a Laguna Indian version, see *Storyteller* by Leslie Marmon Silko (New York: Little, Brown & Co., 1981).

The *Lutin* and the Hay Wagon

Translated and adapted from a story told by Émile Lévesque of Augusta, Maine, collected by Claire Violette, and deposited in 1968 in the Archives of Oral History and Folklore of the University of Maine, Orono, this story was published in *D'la boucane* by Julien Olivier (Cambridge, Massachusetts.: National Assessment and Dissemination Center, 1979). Our thanks to Dr. Sandy Ives for permission to use this material—again.

Variants of "mischievous little people" and "fairies borrowing" tales are widespread—from the well-known leprechauns and fairies of the British Isles to various Oriental imps and elves. The *lutins'* speciality of borrowing farmers' horses appears to be unique to these "little people" of Québec.

The *Chasse-Galerie*

This story was translated and freely adapted from the traditional tale published in the late nineteenth century by Honoré

Beaugrand in *La chasse galerie*, first in French (a copy of which was used for the present adaptation), then in English (in the *Century Magazine*). It was reprinted by E.Z. Massicotte in *Conteurs Canadiens Français au XIXe Siècle* (Montréal: Librairie Beauchemin, Limitée, 1908). Massicotte says that the tale was brought over from France and adapted to Canada by the trappers and *coureurs de bois*. Beaugrand, a journalist and novelist who lived in New Orleans and Fall River, Massachusetts, before returning to Québec and becoming mayor of Montréal, attributes the story's survival in the New World to the men of the Northwest territories. It was perpetuated, he said, by French-Canadian woodsmen whom, he adds, "often told him themselves that had seen canoes filled with men off to see their girlfriends." Noted folklorist Marius Barbeau points out in *L'Arbre des Rêves* (Montréal: Éditions Lumen, 1947) that additional information can be found in the *Journal of American Folklore* (July-Sept., 1920). This story was also featured in a 1945 CBC broadcast of *Canadian Yarns*.

French-Canadians and Franco-Americans regard the *Chasse-Galerie* as one of the best known legends of their oral tradition. The story's variations have several constant elements. Travelers who always want to go quickly from one place to another enlist the aid of the Devil, who takes them to their destination in a birch-bark canoe. They cannot let the name of God cross their lips during the voyage and must avoid striking the cross of a church steeple as they fly. They also must agree to deliver their immortal souls to the Devil if they do not fulfill the first two conditions. Twentieth-century versions refer to flying machines more technologically advanced than the birch-bark canoe. The most recent reference seen by the authors is a 1977 cartoon in which the passengers lament that they "should have been more careful in selecting a small, cut-rate airline."

The String of Trout
This story was translated and adapted from a story told by Mrs. Daniel Poirier (Delia Gallant) of Prince Edward Island—the smallest Canadian province, an island east of New Brunswick, separated from the mainland by the Northumberland Strait—collected by Luc Lacourcière, and found at the Archives de Folklore of the Université Laval, recording #3388.

The priest's position in a typical nineteenth-century Québec village is central to understanding this story. The priest, also known as a *curé*, was not only a spiritual leader but also a counselor to the troubled, a moral arbiter, a mediator of domestic disputes, as well as a literate person who often helped illiterate villagers with official, written communications. He was, by far, the most important, powerful, and, usually, the most respected person in the community. Thus, the boy's actions and words take on a greater weight.

Variants of this tale involving "repartee based on church or clergy" are numerous in French Canada. The main characters are usually an overbearing priest and a boy, who manages to deal a clever blow to the priest's pomposity. In a story called "The Intelligent Little Boy," the priest tests the child by inviting him to dinner with a group of fellow priests. They tell him to serve himself first, but that they will do to him whatever he does to the chicken. After pondering the possibilities, he sticks a finger into the opening, pulls out some stuffing, and licks it off his finger.

Justice is Blind

This story was translated and adapted from a story told by Alexandre Poudrier of Yamachiche, Québec, to Adelard Lambert, collected by Marius Barbeau and published in *Les rêves des chasseurs* (The Dreams of the Hunters) (Montréal: Éditions Beauchemin, 1945).

Écu in the Middle Ages—and in heraldry today—was a shield. Here, it means an ancient coin bearing the engraving of a shield and usually worth three *livres* (pounds). In the early 1990s, the ECU became the common monetary exchange of the European Union.

Variants of "The Lawyer's Mad Client" tale include the French tale "The Three Butchers from Reims" and folktales from as far away as Nigeria.

The Indian and the Pastor

Michael's father, Gérard Parent, told him this story. Somewhat similar to "String of Trout," it is part of a large body of stories found in France, Russia, and many other parts of the world, where a lowly person ridicules the all too-powerful representative of the already powerful church.

The Secret of the Animals

This story was translated and adapted from a story in *Il était une fois* (Once Upon a Time) (Montréal: Éditions Beauchemin, 1935) by

Marius Barbeau and Adelard Lambert, who spent a good part of his life in New Hampshire.

The Norwegian tale "True and Untrue" is a very close variant of this tale. Renowned folklorist Stith Thompson points out that this is "one of the oldest and best known of folktales (found) in Oriental and Medieval literature."

Little Thumbkin

This story is translated and adapted from a story in *Il était une fois* (Once Upon a Time) by Marius Barbeau and Adelard Lambert (Montréal: Éditions Beauchemin, 1935).

Dinner was the noon meal.

In French and English, the mother is *porteuse*, a bearer. Poucet's play on word suggests carrying both a load and a child. *Mettre bas*, or to put ... down, is another play on words suggesting "to place on the ground," but also "to give birth" (as to an animal).

The most obvious variant of this tale is the Brothers Grimm's "Tom Thumb."

The Poor Man's Bean

This story is translated and adapted from *Contes de bûcherons* (Lumberjack Tales) by Jean-Claude Dupont (Montréal: Les Quinze, Editeur, 1980). The authors thank Professor Dupont for permission to use this and other tales he has collected and published.

The beanstalk to heaven is an interesting combination of folk and religious elements. The "back road from heaven" is a feature not often found in folktales.

At the end of the version Michael and Julien worked from, the stick does beat the nagging wife. They decided, however, that the point could be made without giving the reader yet another instance of violence against women.

The Italian tale, "The Ass that Lays Money," is a close variant. Another Italian tale, "Jump Into My Sack," as well as the British "Jack and the Beanstalk," are somewhat less similar variants.

The Bear and the Fox

Translated and adapted from a story told by Achille Fournier of Sainte-Anne-de-la-Pocatière, Kamouraska, Québec, this story was published in *Il Était une Fois* (Once Upon a Time) by Marius Barbeau and Adelard Lambert (Montréal: Éditions Beauchemin, 1935).

This story is similar to countless Br'er Rabbit stories, Coyote stories, and other trickster tales from folk traditions all over the world.

The Friend of Thieves

This story was translated and adapted from a story told by Adelard Lambert of Yamachiche, Québec, collected by Marius Barbeau and published in *Grand'mère Raconte* (Grandmother Tells Stories) (Montréal: Éditions Beauchemin, 1935).

Similiar to a trickster story, it conveys the idea of "no honor among thieves." It is also similiar to "Justice is Blind" and "The Two Magicians" in this collection.

Ivory Mountain

Translated and adapted from a story told by Jean-Yves Bigras of Ottawa in 1930, this story was collected and published by Marius Barbeau in *Le miroir qui parle* (The Talking Mirror) (Montréal: Les Éditions Chantecler, 1953).

Lieue, or league, is an ancient measure equaling about 2.5 miles or four kilometers. It is well-known in the French tales *Les bottes de sept lieues* (The Seven League Boots) and *Vingt mille lieues sous les mers*, Jules Verne's *20,000 Leagues under the Sea*. This measurement was used in France long before the metric system. It was brought to New France and found a permanent place in French-Canadian literature.

The Swedish story, "The Princess Who Was Rescued from Slavery" is a distant variant. Stith Thompson says it is a —form of the Grateful Dead Man story, particularly well-known in northern Europe.

Drip-Nose and Golden Fish

Translated and adapted from a story told by Jean-Yves Bigras of Ottawa in 1930, this story was collected by Adelard Lambert, ca. 1930, and published by Marius Barbeau in *Le miroir qui parle* (The Talking Mirror) (Montréal: Les Éditions Chantecler, 1953).

Morvette is the main character's name in French. It could be translated more literally, graphically, and perhaps accurately as "Snot-Nose." Michael decided Drip-Nose would serve the purpose and present less of a distraction.

Variants include the Russian tale "The Fool and the Magic Fish" and the Armenian story of "The Talking Fish."

The Two Magicians

Translated and adapted from a story told in 1915 by Achille Fournier of Sainte-Anne-de-la-Pocatière, Kamouraska, Québec, this story was published in *Il Était une Fois* (Once Upon a Time) by Marius Barbeau and Adelard Lambert (Montréal: Éditions Beauchemin, 1935).

Pristi is a traditional French Canadian exclamation meaning literally, in English, *sacristy,* but with the emotional value of *dammit.* It is an excellent example of a universal phenomenon, the corruption of a word when the original is socially unacceptable. *Pristi* is short for *sapristi,* a corruption of *sacristie* (i.e., sacristy, the area adjacent to the altar and church proper where the priest vests), which is a true "swear word" but of a lower order than, let's say, words designating items used for the sacred cult itself or, even worse, the saints or God. All this "profanity" is understandable only in the context of a people well-versed in and appreciative of things religious, liturgical, and theological, but often incomprehensible to others. To each, their own "profanity."

The *pistole* was an ancient gold coin, used in Spain, Italy, and France, and it has an interesting history. At one time in France, the *pistole* was worth ten francs, but that was after the creation of the franc in 1803, and most likely long after the telling of this story in French Canada. Alluding to the firearm imprinted on it, Webster says of *pistole:* "So named in Fr., after a debasement of the coin, in punning allusion to a double use of the original name of the coin, *écu,* which also meant *shield.*"

Reared presented an interesting problem for translation. The French reads se mâta, which at first glance and in the context of a horse story sounds like mater, to tame. However, in the story there is an accent on the *a* (â) and the verb is moreover pronominal *(se).* Moreover, the horse becomes wild, and not tame. What then of *mâter,* to put up a mast? *Voilà!* The horse reared like a mast on a ship, an expression all the more interesting because this maritime origin resembles that of other words and expressions in the traditional French-Canadian and Acadian vocabulary.

The magic horse "had the devil in him" *(le diable au corps),* literally, the devil in his body. This is usually a common enough expression having nothing to do with the supernatural but indicating great movement, or agitation, as in a child. Here, of course, the meaning is more literal and sinister.

The horse "let out a string of farts" *(lança des pétarades)*. As all farmers know, this is a common enough event when a horse or a donkey rears or kicks. *Pétarade* is more commonly used today for sounds coming from the rear of a motorized vehicle—a backfire.

The Baker Gets Rich
This story is translated and adapted from a story told by Achille Fournier to Adelard Lambert of Berthier-en-Haut, Québec, and published in *Il Était une Fois* (Once Upon a Time) by Marius Barbeau and Adelard Lambert (Montréal: Éditions Beauchemin, 1935).

Two similar variants include the Appalachian "Jack and the Robbers" and the German "Bremen Town Musicians."

The Talking Mirror
Translated and adapted from the title story collected by Adelard Lambert, this story was published by Marius Barbeau in *Le miroir qui parle* (The Talking Mirror) (Montréal: Les Éditions Chantecler, 1953).

Similar to the Grimm Brothers' "Snow White,"this story is also known as "Snowdrop" and "Lisa," found in the Italian "Pentamerone" by Basile.

Ti-Jean, Mama, and the Collector
This story is adapted and expanded from a story told to Michael by Ron Evans.

Actually, Ti-Jean said three *Je vous salue Marie,* but one can presume that in either language this traditional prayer had the same purpose. This story is a bit of a mystery. According to Michael and Julien, they have never found it in print, nor have they heard of a similar tale.

Words Into Flowers
This story is translated and adapted from a story told by Mrs. Prudent Sioui (Marie Picard), a *métis* of the Huron people of Lorette, Québec, collected by Marius Barbeau and published in *Grand-mère Raconte* (Grandmother Tells Stories) (Montréal: Éditions Beauchemin, 1935).

Variants of this story are known throughout the world. There's "Cinderella" (German), "Cendrillon" (France), "The Two Stepsisters" (Norwegian), "Vasilisa the Beautiful" (Russia), "The Goose Girl" (German).

The White Cat

Translated and adapted from a story told in 1915 by Joseph Patry of Saint-Victor, Québec, to Adelard Lambert, this story was collected by Marius Barbeau and published in *Les rêves des chasseurs* (The Dreams of the Hunters) (Montréal: Éditions Beauchemin, 1945).

St. John's fires, or *les feux de la Saint-Jean*, is a tradition still very much alive today. Its origins can be traced not only to Canada but to the Middle Ages in France, and before that, to pre-Christian Gaul. It was originally a celebration of the summer solstice. Many of the celebration's traditions remain the same today, including song, dance, prayer for the summer planting, and the traditional bonfire, a symbol of the returning sun.

The King Makes a Proclamation

This story was translated and adapted from a story told in 1914 by Mrs. Prudent Sioui (Marie Picard) of Lorette, Québec, collected and published by Marius Barbeau in *Le miroir qui parle* (The Talking Mirror) (Montréal: Les Éditions Chantecler, 1953).

Ti-Jean slices off the three giants' heads as they come through the tunnel into the castle. So the reader might logically ask why we've chosen not to make a textual change in this case as we did in a previous story, *Ti-Jean Dry Bread*. In the case of *The King Makes a Proclamation*, Ti-Jean has a limited range of choices since the giants are awake, alert, and feverishly close to their goal. In *Ti-Jean Dry Bread*, the giants are unconscious, and the hero has thus more options for incapacitating them.

Pierre and the Chain Saw

This story is considered a regional joke, expanded by Michael. Ethnic jokes commenting on a certain group's alleged backwardness or stupidity are found in every culture.

The Shoemaker and the Spinner

This story was translated and adapted from a story told by Philéas Bédard of Saint-Rémi de Napierville, Québec, collected by Marius Barbeau, and published in 1935 by Barbeau and Adelard

Lambert in *Il était une fois* (Once Upon a Time) (Montréal: Éditions Beauchemin, 1935).

When the shoemaker speaks to his wife in French, he endearingly calls her *ma vieille* which, in English, transliterates as *my old*. If that sounds incomplete in English, it's because we expect to hear *old something—woman*, for example. And so, we used old woman in the story, realizing full well that *old woman* has negative connotations never intended by the shoemaker, although it was our best option. Both *ma vieille* and its male equivalent, *mon vieux* are, in French, well-known expressions of endearment. Later, when the shoemaker is referred to as *son vieux* (literally, *her old*), we felt that *her old man* would be too misleading. thus we translated with the more neutral word *husband*.

The king says that "two more or less are not going to make any difference." The concluding phrase attempts to render the original *N'est pas la mer à boire*. This popular saying means literally *is not the ocean to drink*—i.e., it's not a big deal!

In the original, what we have translated as *flour* is said to be *de la fleur*, which means, literally, *some flower* (the plant). *Fleur* does not mean *flour* (the baking ingredient). The standard French for *flour* is *farine*. So where does the confusion come from? The use of *fleur* (the plant) is a mistaken Anglicisation, one not uncommon among older French-Canadians and Franco-Americans.

Crêpes are thin pancakes, a staple both in France, particularly in Normandy, and among French-heritage people in North America. The closest translation is pancake, but a *crêpe* is no more a pancake than a *tortilla* is a pancake.

"To heck with you!" says the old man. In French, he said *Bernique*, lit., "limpet" (a shell fish). *Bernique* is most likely a diminutive, suggesting another word that is closer to profanity, albeit a toned-down version of something worse. Profanity in the French-Canadian tradition is often related to religious items and subjects. Julien's etymological conjecture for *bernique* is the following: it's a "hidden form of *'bernacle*, which is a diminutive of *tabernacle*, a heavy-duty and quite commonly used "swear word."

The stranger is looking for Fifth Row (*Le Cinquième Rang*). The best farms were by the river, especially the Saint Lawrence River. Beyond these chosen spots were *rangs*, roads or "rows." The further from Row One, the more one was in the country.

Regarding Poverty-Place, the French, *Goutte-Pouille,* suggests a place dripping either with lice or injuries. To be on the Fifth Row of Poverty Place is about as bad as things can get.

This tale, similar to the Russian tale "Foolish Wife, Foolish Husband" is a variant of the "chattering woman" theme. The twist that the man is the one who cannot hold his tongue is not unique to this story.

Montréal Hockey
This is an old, French-Canadian joke.

Cricket the Smartest Figure-Outer
Émile Lévesque of Augusta, Maine, along with the Archives of Folklore and Oral History at the University of Maine at Orono were sources for this tale. See *D'la boucane* (For more details, see "The *Lutins* and the Hay Wagon.") and *Criquette* by Julien Olivier and Normand C. Dubé (Cambridge, Mass.: Lesley College, 1980).

For versions from Louisiana, see "Cricket is Caught" in *Folk Tales from French Louisiana* (Baton Rouge: Clator's Publishing, 1962) and "The Diviner," in *Fools and Rascals,* by Calvin Andre Claudel (Lafayette, La.: Legacy Publishing Co., 1978). The story is easily recognizable despite the slightly different elements.

A note on the three meals. In telling this story, Julien tries to make the meals as appetizing as possible to a given audience. Turkey, dressing, and ice cream smorgasbord for some, meatless tofu salad and rice for others, or maybe gumbo, *tourtière* (meat pie), *crêpes,* and *tarte au sucre* (sugar pie).

The French title to this story, *Fin devineur par-dessus fin devineur,* is difficult to translate. *Fin devineur* ... has meaning and rhythm not conveyed in English. A combination magician, fortune teller, and wise person, a *devineur* is not quite a magician nor a mere diviner. He is smart and figures things out, thus Julien's preference for "Figure-outer." Cricket has a lot of native intelligence—unschooled basic smarts. He is really Ti-Jean with a name change.

When Cricket has enjoyed each meal, he says, "Well, there's the first (second, third) one!" In French, *"Voilà le premier ... de pris!"* has a play on words, with *pris* meaning both *taken* (as in a meal) and *captured* (as in a crook).

Cricket's deception to attain riches or to increase his social stature is a story type similar to "Ti-Jean and the Elite" and the

German tale "Tyll Eulenspiegel the Doctor." The cricket character is also found in stories in Cajun folklore, as well as in Russian tales.

D'Amours the Fastest Runner in the World

This story was told by Émile Lévesque of Augusta, Maine, and can also be found in the Archives of Folklore and Oral History at UMO; *D'la boucane*. (For details, see "The *Lutin* and the Hay Wagon.")

The Lévesques were from Trois-Pistoles, a Québec town on the south shore of the Saint Lawrence River about one-hundred and eighty miles upstream from the city of Québec. The area is called *Bas St-Laurent* or Lower Saint Lawrence. This story reminds us that back in those days when farms were far apart and communication was difficult, the time after church on Sunday was dedicated to gossip, business, and for contacting people.

D'Amours literally means "of loves." It is a common family name.

Stories with main characters who possess amazing, even absurd, physical powers are found everywhere. Paul Bunyon, Mike Fink, and a host of great swimmers, warriors, sharpshooters, and runners are only the beginning of a very long list of such characters.

Books and Audiocassettes from August House Publishers

See Rock City
A Journey Through Appalachia
Donald Davis
Hardback $22.95 / ISBN 0-87483-448-1
Paperback $12.95 / ISBN 0-87483-456-2
Audiobook $12.00 / ISBN 0-87483-452-X

The Farm on Nippersink Creek
Stories from a Midwestern Childhood
Jim May
Hardback $18.95 / ISBN 0-87483-339-6
Paperback $12.95 / ISBN 0-87483-446-5
Audiobook $18.00 / ISBN 0-87483-419-8

Still Catholic After All These Fears
Ed Stivender
Hardback $19.95 / ISBN 0-87483-403-1
Paperback $11.95 / ISBN 0-87483-483-X

Ready-To-Tell Tales
Sure-fire Stories from America's Favorite Storytellers
David Holt and Bill Mooney
Hardback $29.95 / ISBN 0-87483-380-9
Paperback $19.95 / ISBN 0-87483-381-7

Cajun Folktales
J.J. Reneaux
Hardback $19.95 / ISBN 0-87483-283-7
Paperback $11.95 / ISBN 0-87483-282-9
Audiobook $12.00 / ISBN 0-87483-383-3

AUGUST HOUSE PUBLISHERS, INC.
P.O. BOX 3223
LITTLE ROCK, AR 72203
1-800-284-8784

MICHAEL PARENT *(left)* is a native of Lewiston, Maine. He graduated from Providence College in Rhode Island and taught high school before deciding to pursue a career as a storyteller, singer, and juggler. He tells original stories and performs stories and songs from the Franco-American tradition and experience. In his spare time, he has explored Calgary and Vancouver on roller blades and helped to start a local theater in Charlottesville, Virginia, where he is now based.

JULIEN OLIVIER *(right)* has researched, written, and lectured extensively on Franco-American history, language, and culture, particularly in the areas of folklore and oral history. An accredited translator, he is owner of Olivier International Communications Services, offering linguistic and cultural services to business, government, and non-profit groups. He lives in Barrington, New Hampshire, with his wife, Jane Duddy Olivier, and their four daughters.